Books by Elizabeth Ashworth
Published by Ulverscroft:

THE DE LACY INHERITANCE
AN HONOURABLE ESTATE

FAVOURED BEYOND FORTUNE

He is rich who has that which his heart desires . . . Married off at thirteen to Thomas of Lancaster, Alicia de Lacy is trapped in a loveless, childless union. Tiring of her, Thomas sends her away into virtual exile, accompanied by the squire Eble le Strange — who secretly carries a torch for her. When her husband leads a rebellion against King Edward II, Alicia — once one of the richest noblewomen in England — loses everything. Everything except the love of one man . . .

Elizabeth Ashworth is an author based in Lancashire. Her work has appeared in many publications, including *My Weekly*, *People's Friend*, *Take a Break Fiction Feast*, *The Lady*, *The Times* and *Top Gear*.

ELIZABETH ASHWORTH

FAVOURED BEYOND FORTUNE

Complete and Unabridged

ULVERSCROFT
Leicester

First published in Great Britain in 2014

First Large Print Edition
published 2015

C46044711$

A catalogue record for this book is available
from the British Library.

ISBN 978-1-4448-2540-4

Published by
F. A. Thorpe (Publishing)
Anstey, Leicestershire

Set by Words & Graphics Ltd.
Anstey, Leicestershire
Printed and bound in Great Britain by
T. J. International Ltd., Padstow, Cornwall

This book is printed on acid-free paper

Prologue

*He is rich who has that which
his heart desires.*

It was the movement that caught my eye. Dark against azure, a figure performed an energetic carole as it danced towards the ground, and I thought that it was beautiful. But when the cry reached me I saw that the figure was neither dancing nor swimming but was grasping at elusive air. Time paused and I gazed upwards for an eternity, eyes dazzled by the sun and my mind seeking explanation. Then I felt the courtyard shake as it thumped the ground. It looked like the doll I held in my hand. Its limbs were twisted as if they were stuffed with rags and it was silent. A woman screamed and others joined until there was a chorus. As my lady mother passed me in a cloud of lavender scent, her skirts raised to show grey stockings, I felt myself lifted skywards and carried into the dimness of the women's chamber by my nurse. It was not until I was much older that I understood what I had witnessed.

John was the second of my brothers to die. My brother Edmund died before I could remember him. No one has ever told me about him, but adults are often indiscreet around the ears of children and I have heard enough snatches of conversation to know that he drowned in the well of Denbigh Castle when those lands were given to my father after the wars with the Welsh. My father had taken the family there that summer to oversee the building of a new stone castle. Edmund had been watching the work when another boy had taken one of the kittens that roamed the courtyard and thrown it down the well. Hearing its futile mewing Edmund had climbed down to rescue it, but had lost his grip on the slippery stones and plunged into the numb-cold water below. The water that was the life-blood of the castle embraced my brother and took him for its own. He was dead before they pulled him out, the kitten still clutched in his grasp, and my father, grieving for his first born son and heir, abandoned the work and brought his family home to Pontefract Castle in Yorkshire, to the high ridge where Ilbert de Lacy had built a fortress two hundred years before.

It was here, in the nursery tower that overlooked the inner bailey, that baby Margaret slipped from this life. All I recall of her was a swaddled bundle that was placed in my arms. She was heavy. Much heavier than my doll.

My mother sat close beside me, outstretched hands waiting to catch the baby should she fall. But I held my little sister tight. Her cheeks were red and the skin flaked away across the grizzled little forehead that showed beneath her bands. Her dark blue eyes sought mine and she stared up at me as if she knew me, and in that moment I loved her. She was a good baby, they said, a quiet babe who never cried. She didn't even cry the night she died. She was too special to remain with us, my nurse gently explained. God had seen fit to take her and surely she would not go to purgatory. For what sins had she committed during her fleeting visit to earth? They lifted her from the wooden cradle, unbound her swaddling, washed her and took her away. She was the first and last baby I have rocked in my arms that I can call my kin.

When John fell from the turret my father said that if he had lived he would have whipped him for being up there. I wondered if John would have preferred that or if he was glad that he was dead, but when I asked my nurse she bade me hold my tongue lest I was punished for such disgraceful talk. So I sat near the window and unbraided and braided the yellow hair that was stuck to the head of my doll and wondered if the weeping would ever cease.

Part One — 1295 to 1311

1

My mother and I were sitting in the window embrasure stitching a new wall hanging. It was a scene of men and women hunting with hawks and hounds and as we worked we made up stories about the people we were embroidering, and I said that the squire in the background, with the small birds in his hand ready to be plucked for roasting, was secretly in love with the lady in the red gown who rode the fine white horse and held a merlin aloft on her wrist.

I remember that the sun was warm as it slanted in through the open window. I had not been paying full attention to my task and although my lady mother plied her needle diligently I had been teasing one of the tabby cats with a length of thread, making it stand up on its hind legs and swipe the air as it tried to grasp the bright blue filament in its sharp claws. My mother was indulgent of me and did not direct me back to my work but paused to laugh at the animal's antics as it overbalanced and fell, then sat up to wash its flanks as if that would restore its dignity.

As we were laughing we heard the horses

and I watched as my father got down from his bay courser and came towards the tower where we were working. It was unusual for him to come to us in the women's solar and my mother quickly put aside her silks and hurried to curtsey before him. I was more leisurely. I knew that if I lingered my father would snatch me up before my greeting was complete and would hug me to him, and that he would smell of sweat and horses and wine, and his moustache would tickle my face as he kissed me. But that day his greeting seemed distracted and his face was flushed a deeper red than just the journey and the heat of the sun could cause.

My mother waved to one of the women to pour wine and she handed the cup to him with an eager face. 'Do you bring good news, my lord?' she asked. She always wanted to hear the latest gossip and she and her women chatted endlessly about any snippet that could be gleaned from the travelling friars who often sat at our dinner table to refresh themselves on their journeys.

She had spent time at court before her marriage and she often told me about the things she had seen and done there. Her eyes took on a faraway glow when she spoke about her youth, as if she was still living it in her mind and it was more real to her than the present. She often talked of the king, Edward, and his queen, Eleanor. She said that they had loved each other very much and one of her favourite stories was about the time when Eleanor had accompanied Edward on crusade to the Holy Land. He had almost been killed by an assassin who struck at him with a poisoned knife and my lady mother told me that Eleanor had sucked the poison from his wounded arm and saved him. I had only vague memories of Queen Eleanor. I was presented to her once when she was at Harby, not far from Lincoln. She died there of a fever and my mother took me to see the tomb in Lincoln Cathedral where her viscera were buried before her preserved body was taken to Westminster. Even then I had thought it an odd practice and as I stood by the shining tomb I had asked my mother how Queen Eleanor would eat her dinner when she reached heaven if only the outer shell of her that was buried in London was raised up on the day of judgement. My mother didn't answer me but shushed me harshly and hurried me out of the cathedral with apologies to the priest who had overheard my words. But it worried me for a long time and I even cried at the thought of Queen Eleanor having to remain hungry for the whole of eternity.

Now my lady mother watched my father with eager eyes as he drank his wine and handed the empty cup to the servant.

'I have spoken with Edmund of Lancaster and he has agreed to the betrothal of his son, Thomas, and our daughter.'

I laid a hand on my father's mud splattered sleeve. 'What is he like? Does he joust?' I asked, thinking of the heroes of the stories that I loved.

My father smiled down and with a warm hand under my chin he kissed my face. 'It is an excellent match for you, Alicia. I could not have found you a better husband. I have agreed that Thomas should join our household,' he told my mother, 'and in two years' time we will host the wedding.'

'But surely that is too soon,' objected my mother. 'At scarce thirteen she will not be ready to be a bride to any man.'

'It is the king's wishes,' replied my father with exasperation. 'He does us honour with this offer of his nephew, and if we hesitate there will be others more than willing to agree to a match with a boy who carries the royal blood of both England and France. Our grandchildren will carry royal blood from both parents and . . . ' He paused with a shrug of his shoulders and turned his face from us. Perhaps he thought of my brother

John and of Edmund, drenched and still, pulled from the well at Denbigh. 'And what other future is there now for the de Lacys?' he asked my lady mother. 'When my wife will bear me no more sons?'

My mother returned to the bench below the window and silently picked up her needle. I thought then that she was angry. Now I understand that it was because she could not endure the pain of loss that she refused my father.

I broke the silent tension with a question. 'What does he look like?' I asked. Was he the courtly knight on the jet black horse that I had prayed to the saints for so diligently? A man who would come to win my hand in marriage as Guarin de Metz had won the hand of the Lady Melette of the White Tower. If he was a nephew to the king then surely he must be tall and well made, with a handsome face and kindly disposition. Though to be truthful I probably never considered his disposition at all. My father was the only man I knew well and at that age I thought all men were as good and kind as him. As I stood there in the solar that day my young thoughts were of nothing more than new clothes, a great feast with music and dancing and a comely man who would hold my hand and look on me with admiration and devotion.

My mother spoke the truth when she said that I was too young, for I knew nothing of what it really meant to be a wife.

I was a girl of eleven summers then and what I thought I knew about love I had gleaned from the ballads that the minstrels sang and the precious books that the women read aloud in my mother's chamber. I heard them all eagerly, not discerning between truth and legend. I believed them and stored them in my imagination to be embellished as I allowed my mind to wander in the dark hours of the night or when my attention should have been more firmly fixed on my work or on my prayers.

Sometimes the women would re-tell the stories when the day's tasks had been done and it grew too dark to sew in the flickering candlelight. If it was not yet time to retire to bed, someone would lay their work aside and begin their favourite story. My mother liked to tell the tale of how Payn Peverel slew the giant Geomagog. But I always hoped that someone would tell my favourite story about Lady Melette. No suitor could find favour with Melette and when her uncle asked her if there was no knight that she would take as her lord, she told him: 'There is no knight that I would take for riches or honours of lands, but if ever I take such a one he shall be handsome, and courteous, and accomplished, and the most valiant of his order in all Christendom. Of riches I make no account, for truly can I say that he is rich who has that which his heart desires.' Her uncle told her that he would do everything in his power to help her find such a lord, and that for a portion he would give her the White Tower with all its fiefs so that she should be sought after for her wealth as well as her beauty. Then, he made a proclamation in many lands and cities that all the knights of worth who would tourney for love should come at the feast of St Michael to the castle of Peverel and that the knight who performed the best should have the hand of the Lady Melette. The tournament was fierce and desperate. Many knights were unhorsed and many hard blows were given and received. Lady Melette and her women watched from a high tower and they saw that Guarin de Metz was the best, the fairest and the most valiant of them all. He was victorious against all comers and to him fell the prize of the tournament — the Lady Mellette. They were wedded within the sight of everyone and when the feast was ended Guarin took his wife and his brothers to the White Town where they stayed for forty days. Then his brothers returned to Brittany, except for the youngest, Guy. He remained in

England and he was called Guy le Strange, and from him are descended all the lords who have that name.

★　★　★

I went to my betrothal with my imagination fuelled by such romantic tales. I believed that when I saw Thomas of Lancaster he too would be handsome and courteous and accomplished and the most valiant of his order in all of Christendom; that he would shine with courtly deeds and goodness and would be to me as Guarin had been to Melette. I had even worked our intertwined initials on a pair of white gloves to present to my betrothed as a gift that he could carry until our wedding day.

Unlike William Peverel my father had not arranged a tourney at Pontefract where knights could fight for my hand in marriage, though he had smiled indulgently when I spoke of Lady Melette. My father was an affectionate man. He would often hold me close against his soft, warm body where my face would mould itself into his flesh and my senses would be lost in the scent of the cedar and rue in which his tunics were stored in the coffer beside the bed where he slept. His lips would press down hard on the top of my head as he whispered, 'You are all I have now, Alicia. You are all I have.'

'Those are only stories,' he had said as he took me on his lap and tugged at my braid to tease me. 'What if some ugly, lame or hunchback knight won your hand? You would not be pleased with me then.'

'How could he win if he were lame or hunchback?' I demanded.

'That does not exclude ugly,' laughed my father and I recall that I could not match his mirth, but clung to his warm tunic and did not know how I would ever manage without him. 'We will have a Round Table to celebrate your wedding,' he promised. 'You will see. Your husband will acquit himself well because I will teach him to be the best knight Pontefract has ever seen. For am I not a great knight myself?' he asked me as he wound my braid around his fingers. I ran my hand over his rotund stomach and wondered if he could still unhorse any opponent in the lists as he claimed he had done when he captained the king's Round Table at Nefyn to celebrate the conquest of the Welsh. I believed that he could.

But as soon as I saw Thomas of Lancaster I knew that he was no Guarin de Metz. I was waiting with my father and mother outside the door to the great hall when he rode into the castle bailey on a plain grey courser beside his father, Edmund, duke of Lancaster and his mother, Blanche of Artois. He took his time dismounting and I felt uncomfortable as I stood and waited for him to hand the reins to a groom. As he approached I saw that he was much taller than me. His hair looked as though it had just been sheared. Whether his face had been shaved I was unsure, although I thought not as there was a fuzz on his upper lip. His features seemed to have sprung from his mother, along with her slightly weak chin, and his expression was one of arrogance as he stared around at the curved walls of the keep and the sturdy towers of the castle. His mouth turned down in petulance and he gazed upon me with disdain as I walked forward to greet him in obedience.

The ground was hard and stony beneath my knees and I hoped that I would not rip the fabric of my new saffron coloured gown with its purple belt, nor tear my delicate stockings as I knelt before him and offered him my palms pressed tightly together between his as a sign of my deference to his will. His hand was clammy around my fingers as he raised me up and there was a slight sound like the whisper of a midnight breeze from the women who watched us. His eyes were a mud brown and just as dull as I tilted up my face for his moist kiss. His breath smelt a little of goose fat and he had an angry red spot on his forehead.

I looked down as befitted a well behaved girl and hoped that it was because he was as overwhelmed as I was by the occasion that he seemed so unfriendly. Surely I could trust my father to have chosen well?

The next day we were betrothed. I had been bathed in water scented with rose petals and other herbs, in a tub lined with linen in the bedchamber. A bath was a special treat and I enjoyed the way the warm water lapped at my body, caressing and warming my skin and softening my fingertips until they were white and crinkled. My hair had been washed with rosemary to make it shine. One of the women had poured the water from a jug whilst I held my head back and pressed a cloth over my face to keep it from my eyes and nose. My mother and my nurse had rubbed me dry before the hearth and dressed me in a new undergown of pure white and a long fitted tunic of blue as a symbol of my purity. My hair was left uncovered and loose as befitted my maidenly virtue and when it was dry they combed and combed it until every dark strand was tamed.

I was not unused to such attentions and I

enjoyed being fussed over. Ever since the day I had watched my brother fall from the turret, everywhere I went there was someone with me. I was never left unattended and the words 'Be careful, Mistress Alicia' followed me like a charm.

When the hour came, my father stood at the door and smiled at the sight of me. He took my hand in his large warm one and my mother took my other hand and they led me out, across the courtyard where all the household had gathered to see me pass and throw herbs at my feet. We walked in the sunshine towards the chapel of St Clement where I would exchange vows and plight troth with my intended husband.

Thomas of Lancaster was standing between his parents at the chapel door. He was staring at the ground and pushing a small stone backwards and forwards with the toe of his pointed leather shoe. As we approached, my father and mother leading me, he looked up and met my eyes with contempt. I hesitated, but my father tugged me gently forward and when I glanced up at him he gave me an encouraging smile.

'Does he not look handsome?' he asked me. I looked again. Thomas was dressed in a long tunic of red samite as Guarin had been in the story that I loved, but it displeased me because the surly boy who stood before me had nothing in common with that hero. I gave him a half smile, but it was not returned and he did not meet my eyes again. His thin lips were pressed closed and his shoulders hunched inside the tunic with its embroidered roses. When the bishop reached for his hand to join it with mine it felt cold and I would have pulled mine away had the bishop not had his fingers clasped firmly around my wrist.

'Will you promise to take this woman as your wife?' he asked and Thomas muttered that he would and I quaked inside to think that I must spend the rest of my life with him. I thought that he looked cruel, the sort of boy who tormented those who were inferior to him for fun. I had seen such boys in my father's household before, though he tried his best to curb such behaviour and I had once seen him strip and beat a young squire for allowing a wound to his dog's paw to fester so badly that it had to be put out of its pain.

'Will you promise to take this man as your husband?' the bishop asked me. I looked at my sad faced mother and then at my father who nodded his head at me enthusiastically, the flecks of grey in his freshly barbered hair catching the light. Silence hung in the morning air like a bad smell as the adults

19

waited for me to give my word.

'I will,' I whispered. For what choice had I but to comply? I gazed towards the high wall that surrounded the inner bailey. I had always thought of it as my friend, whose loving embrace kept me safe from myriad dangers that lurked on the other side — the evil spirits like the fallen angel who lived in the body of Geomagog. But at that moment I saw that the high walls were my prison and that it was not a giant with a huge club that I needed to fear but the long limbed boy who stood beside me and who would be my lord and have command over me.

2

As his company rode northwards to join the court at Berwick, Henry watched Thomas of Lancaster who was riding ahead of him. Had he done the right thing, he asked himself once more, by betrothing Alicia to him. Looked at coldly the deal that the king had laid before him had seemed too good to refuse, but during the six months that the boy had been in his household he had begun to have doubts about him. From the outset Thomas had seemed to believe that he was superior to the other squires. He seemed to think that it was beneath him to pick up a fork and clear the dung from the stables or sit on an upturned bucket and polish harness with vigour. His riding skills were poor to say that he had been raised with every opportunity to become an excellent horseman and, though his own opinion of his capabilities was high, Henry found him disappointing in many ways. Still, he thought, the lad was only young and perhaps he had been pampered too much. Though, heaven knows, he thought, he had tried his best to give his own sons a sense of independence and look where that had led.

Henry shook his head to try to rid his inner eye of the disturbing image of his unhappy daughter. Thomas showed no interest in Alicia whatsoever and when they were together he was offhand almost to the point of rudeness. Henry would have dismissed it as adolescent embarrassment, but he knew that Thomas was old enough and mature enough to be interested in other girls. Although he had tried to convince himself that he had not seen the boy kissing and fondling one of the laundress's daughters he knew that it had happened and would probably happen again. He wasn't sure what to do. If it had been one of the other squires he would have smiled to himself and made a mental note to take him aside and warn him of the dangers that such meddling might bring. The reminder that bastard children sprung from such couplings and would need to be provided for was often lesson enough to make the boys at least careful in their pleasure taking. But how was he to approach such a matter with the boy who was to marry his own daughter?

Henry tried to dismiss the problem from his mind for the present. He had an important role to fulfil at Berwick and he must try to give it his whole attention.

'Is all well, my lord?' asked his friend, Miles de Stapleton, as he drew his dappled gelding alongside him.

'Aye. I was merely lost in thought,' he replied as he leaned to smooth his horse's mane to one side of its muscular neck, 'about the new ruler of the Scots.'

'What do you think of John Balliol?' asked Miles.

'He'll be more biddable than Bruce,' said Henry. He pulled his mantle more closely around his shoulders as the wind from the east pushed its stealthy fingers under the folds of its fur lining. 'Though heaven knows the discussions have gone on long enough,' he remarked as he turned to urge the remainder of his men on at a faster pace.

At last they saw the high walls rising in the distance around the square keep. The stonework looked greyer than ever in the fading November light and Henry could have sworn that the rain that was lashing against them had a touch of stinging sleet in it. The men were tired and the horses were tired and he acknowledged that Margaret had probably been right when she had pleaded that she did not have the strength for such a journey. She had faded from the happy, obliging woman whom he had loved into a pale ghost who drifted almost unseen around the chambers at Pontefract. He sometimes came across her staring from the window that overlooked the inner bailey and he knew that she was watching the place where John had died. It irritated him. He grieved the loss of their children as well, but life moved on and there were important affairs to attend to. Now that the Welsh had been subjugated, the matter of Scotland had to be addressed and King Edward was determined that he should be acknowledged as their overlord and that the whole of Britain should be united under his rule.

Torches had been lit to welcome them in and as they clopped wearily across the wooden bridge Henry offered up a silent prayer of thanks for their safe arrival in Scotland. His legs were stiff when he slid from his saddle and he stood shaking them a little to try to restore the feeling so that he could walk rather than shuffle into the great hall. The king was waiting inside to receive his greeting. He looked enviably warm and dry as Henry rose from one knee and his old friend clasped his hand.

'By God, man, you're as cold as the grave!' exclaimed Edward. 'Come to the fire and warm your old bones whilst the servants bring in your baggage. Wine for the Earl of Lincoln!' he commanded and Henry drank gratefully as the heat from the flames warmed his face.

'Wife not come?' asked Edward.

'She sends her apologies. She is unwell.'

'No matter. It's not women's work we have to do here,' said the king. 'Though a soft, warm body for the bed is no bad thing these autumn nights.'

Margaret had not warmed Henry's bed since John's death. He remembered how he had gone to her that night, seeking comfort. After Edmund had drowned at Denbigh they had held and comforted one another. When they no longer had any words and could find no answer to the question 'why?' they had succumbed to physical comfort and he had loved his wife tenderly to give them both relief from their relentless tears. But after John's death, Margaret had shuddered at the sight of him and pulled her linen gown tightly closed around her neck as if by doing so she would deny him access to her body. And he had not forced her. God knows, there had been enough pain already.

When the wine was drunk and his squires had brought in the packs from the mules, Henry was shown to his chambers where a page helped him to ease off his boots and put on clean, dry hose. He washed his hands and face and combed his hair and beard with care before going down to the hall to eat. As he made his way down the twisting stone steps, his stomach groaning with hunger and his mouth watering in response to the aromas that were drifting upwards, it wasn't just the need for food that was on his mind. Whilst he was away from his wife he wondered if there might be an opportunity to feed some of his other physical desires as well.

He paused at the entrance to the hall and listened to the hubbub. There were few women in attendance and it was the noise of men's voices, laughing and shouting greetings to one another, that bounced off the stone walls and filled the huge space. The woman he sought was seated close to the top table. She was tucking a loose strand of hair into the elaborate net that covered her head and as he watched she looked up and met his eye. Lady Isabella de Vescy, the young widow of his friend John, inclined her head in greeting. He would speak to her before she retired to bed for the night. Surely there could be no guilt attached to seeking her out to enquire how she fared, he thought. But guilt seemed to assail him. He knew that it was sinful to even think of being untrue to his wife, but he could imagine very well gently taking that net from Isabella's head and allowing her long hair to fall loose. Henry felt himself swell in anticipation. Yes, it was sinful, and although he had not taken any other woman in the year since Margaret had denied him her bed, he wanted Isabella de Vescy with a passion that he knew he could not control.

When the leisurely courses of the meal had been eaten and the leftovers taken away to be distributed at the castle gates to the poor, Henry stood up and stretched his legs. The servants were waiting to stack the trestles against the wall and make the hall ready for the morning so Henry nodded his thanks towards them, pressed a coin into the palm of the one who had been especially attentive to his needs and threaded his way through the throng towards her.

'My lady.'

'My lord,' she replied as she curtseyed.

'I hope I find you well?'

'I am very well, my lord.'

'And are you happy at court?'

'Yes, my lord. The king shows me much kindness and I want for nothing.'

'Nothing?' Her eyes met his as she looked up. They were as dark as Margaret's were pale and the contrast was striking. He couldn't discern their exact colour in the candlelight; he was unsure if they were brown or as blue as a midnight summer sky. He did however notice the blush that burned on her cheeks.

Was it, he hoped, a sign that his feelings might be reciprocated. 'You do know that if there is anything I can do for you, you need only ask me,' he said, wondering if he was pressing his suit too openly.

'I know that I can rely on you to have my welfare in mind,' she replied. 'How long will you remain at court?'

'For a week or so at least,' he told her, 'though I do not want to be trapped here if the weather worsens.' He was about to say that he did not like to leave his wife alone for too long, that he feared for her wellbeing, but the words died on his tongue as she nodded.

'Then I hope you will seek me out again.'

'I will, my lady,' he promised, and as an awkward silence grew between them he nodded his head and found himself walking away from her, cursing himself for a fool.

Back in his chambers as he prepared for bed Henry glimpsed John le Strange waiting outside the door. The man seemed eager to speak to him and his first thought was that he was bringing news of yet more trouble in the marches. It would not be surprising, he thought, if rebels had made use of England's preoccupation with the matters of the Scottish king to grasp what opportunities they could along the Welsh borders. But it turned out to be on a more personal matter that his friend approached him.

'Forgive me for disturbing you,' began John le Strange as Henry gestured to his page to fill cups with wine.

'I would welcome some moments of distraction as long as you do not bring sour news,' remarked Henry. 'Pray reassure me that all is well with my lands in Wales.'

'I have heard nothing to the contrary, my lord,' John le Strange reassured him. 'It is on another matter that I crave a few moments of your time.'

'Speak then,' said Henry, 'whilst I try to recall if I owe you a favour.'

'My youngest son will soon celebrate his eighth birthday and I am seeking a place for him in a household where I know he will be treated kindly,' he said.

'I had not realised your family was so grown. Time passes quickly as the years go on,' remarked Henry. 'And what of your other sons?' he asked.

'John and Hamon are both already placed, amidst their mother's tears. I would have sought a place for Eble too when he reached his seventh birthday but my wife pleaded to keep him a little longer. I see she favours him,' said John. 'He will cause you no trouble, but he will miss his mother's affection and I thought that the countess . . . '

He paused and Henry saw that familiar awkwardness that overcame people when they spoke of their own sons and remembered that he too had once had sons.

'And you would trust me with your boy?' he asked, knowing that others had sent their sons elsewhere, probably thinking that a man who had lost both his own heirs in tragic accidents was not the best guardian of their offspring.

'Yes,' said John firmly. 'I would not ask you otherwise. You are the first I have approached on this matter.'

Henry took a sip of the red wine and wiped his mouth on the back of his hand. 'Bring him to me at Pontefract when we are finished here,' he said. 'If I like what I see and my wife is agreeable then he may stay.'

'Then I will be in your debt, my lord,' replied John and as they sat and drank together their conversation turned to the events of the day and Henry thought no more about young Eble le Strange until the boy was duly delivered into his care.

3

Eble le Strange stood at the edge of the tiltyard with the other boys, feeling a mixture of fear and anticipation. He had been pleased and excited when his father had told him that the Earl of Lincoln had accepted him and he had counted off the days in his head as the preparations were completed. He had been measured for a quilted aketon and new boots. He had gone to the market at Knockin with his mother, and two squires to carry all the packages. They had bought more than enough cloth to sew two changes of linen and several tunics for every day, as well as one for more formal occasions. He had chosen a new cloak and a hood in dark blue and everything had been carefully folded and packed into a small oak coffer in readiness for his departure. His father had bought him a new knife with an engraved handle to take to table and his nurse had combed his head with painful vigour to ensure that no lice lingered there.

At last the morning had come and when it was time to leave he had been eager to leap up into the saddle of Madog, the pony he was taking with him, and he had wriggled self-consciously from his mother's last embrace as she had bade him to be good, to work hard, and to do as he was bid. The birds had been singing their spring songs, the sun was rising higher in the sky and with its warmth on his face he had kicked the flanks of his pony and ridden out of the castle courtyard without a backward glance. His childhood was over and he was going to Pontefract to learn to be a man.

But after his father had ridden away and left him with these strangers, and after he had lain awake in a strange bed, listening to the snorting and snoring of the other boys who shared his chamber, he did not feel so confident or brave. He had been shaken awake at sunrise and after dressing had been given a drink of small ale before being taken to the stables where the harness was stored and given an oiled cloth with which to scrub a hauberk until not a speck of rust remained. He had worked diligently until his arm ached and by the time the bell was rung for dinner his stomach was rumbling in hunger and his new linen was damp with the perspiration of his efforts. He had meekly followed the others to wash his hands and take his seat on a bench at the bottom of the great hall.

'Because you are new you will be served

today,' said the older boy who had been instructed to take care of him until he learnt his way around. 'But one of the roles you will be required to learn is the serving and waiting at table so pay good attention.'

Eble had nodded and watched carefully, although none of it was new to him; he had served at table in his father's household since he was old enough to carry a platter. He had eaten his meal quietly whilst listening to the banter of the other boys, noticing that there was another boy who, like him, was new and sat in silence. His name was John de Warenne and he hoped that they might become friends.

Now, as they stood in the tiltyard to begin their afternoon lesson, the earl of Lincoln was roundly chastising some of the older boys for their unruly behaviour.

'The tournament may be a sport but it is not a game to be taken lightly,' he told them angrily. 'Do not think that a Round Table, where you dress in the colours of the knights of King Arthur to impress the ladies, is the only form of tournament that you will be required to attend.' He glowered at the slight snigger that arose. 'In a real tournament where there is a melee, perhaps one fought with weapons à outrance, you will need all the skills of battle. You will learn what to expect in real combat — the cracking of your teeth, the sight of your own blood, the blows and the unhorsings. If you are to learn the craft of a knight then you must work hard and pay heed to what you are told.'

As Eble watched the red-faced earl glare at the subdued squires he hoped that no one was going to receive a beating. He felt his chin wobble and he bit his lip hard. It would do him no good to be nicknamed a cry baby on his first day in the lists. He felt an increasing urge to visit the latrine but dared not ask permission and he said a silent prayer to the holy mother that he should not piss his hose in the sight of everyone.

He glanced at the boy, John, who stood beside him and saw him wipe his nose on the knuckles of his bare hand. The older boys were still shuffling their feet, but the earl had finished his speech and his face was returning to a paler hue.

'Now, Gilbert and Roger, to your horses and listen well to Sir Miles. If I hear of any more mischief then I'll whip your buttocks so you'll not wish to sit in a saddle for a week!'

Eble felt the warm rush between his thighs and guiltily he moved away from the damp patch in the sand where he was standing, pulling his tunic down and hoping that no one had noticed. When he saw the earl coming towards him he was sure that he was about to receiving a beating himself for his misdemeanour and he shook as the man's hand weighed heavily on his shoulder.

'No need to look so fearful, young Eble,' said the earl. 'You will soon become accustomed to our ways.'

'Y . . . yes, my lord,' he managed to say as the earl moved on to speak to the other boy.

'And you John? Are you finding your way around?'

'Yes, my lord,' he replied. And although the other boy sounded equally afraid he had not lost control of his bladder, thought Eble, as his cheeks burned with shame.

The earl told them to come and watch as Thomas of Lancaster galloped down the lists and tried to take a circlet of rope from a post onto the tip of his blunted lance. He missed it at his first attempt. His face filled with anger and his curse echoed across the lists as he pulled too hard upon the horse's bit to slow the animal. He turned for a second try but dug the spurs too hard into its flanks. It leapt forward, out of control, and as he began the run Eble saw that he would miss again. He leaned from the saddle and stabbed with the lance, but the loop was left swinging on the pole and he cursed at the horse.

'Tis no use blaming old Clarent,' the earl

told him. 'He knows his job well enough and could teach you a thing or two if you would let him.'

'What does a horse know except to obey?' demanded Lancaster as the earl took the reins and soothed the patient gelding by stroking its nose down to its muzzle which was spotted with froth from its foaming mouth.

'Get down now,' he said. 'We'll leave this until another day when you and the horse are calmer.'

'But I know I can do it. Let me have another chance,' said Lancaster, showing no inclination to do as he was bid.

'Get down and take the horse to the stables — and make sure that you rub him down. Don't leave it to a groom. And don't let him drink until he's cool,' said the earl as Lancaster led the horse away with a sulky expression, glaring at Eble and John as he passed.

★ ★ ★

I was at the far end of the stable when Thomas came in. My mare had tripped when I was out riding that morning and although the groom had promised that he would attend to the cut on her knee, and I knew he would, I had gone to check it was done. I was bent down examining her leg when I heard Thomas lead the old chestnut gelding in. The horse was even older than me, but it knew its job in the lists and my father used it to train his young squires.

Thomas didn't see me and something about his face made me reluctant to speak. He seemed angry and as he pulled the saddle from the horse's back his dog, which had been milling around his legs tripped him and he fell heavily into the straw. I couldn't help but let out a squeak of mirth though Thomas, as he struggled to his feet, did not appear to find anything to laugh at.

The dog cringed as he struck it with his whip and a line of fresh blood sprang from its grey coat as it yelped. I wished that it would twist from his grasp and sink its sharp white teeth into his arm but it merely quivered with its tail between its legs and looked up at him with puzzled eyes, not knowing what it had done wrong.

Thomas saw me watching him and held my gaze as he tucked the whip into his belt. 'It needed discipline,' he said as he handed the reins of the horse to a groom and grasped the dog by its collar to take it out of the stable. Its eyes met mine, and in that moment I understood that we were kindred spirits.

'Papa,' I said when I had crept along the wall of the chamber where he was sitting at a desk, moving tally sticks from left to right and carefully checking the figures that had been written on the parchment by his clerk. He grunted and I wasn't sure if he had heard me. He was absorbed in his task and probably did not want to be disturbed. But he always made time for me. I was indulged and I was confident that whatever I asked of him he would grant, so I leaned close to him with my hand resting on his shoulder and after a moment he sat up straight and with a smile he turned to kiss my cheek. 'Papa,' I said again. 'I do not wish to marry Thomas of Lancaster.'

I watched as his smile faded to be replaced by a frown. 'What is done cannot be undone, Alicia,' he told me quietly.

'But, Papa, I do not like him,' I said, surprised that my father would deny my request to be released from my betrothal.

'Alicia.' He put a strong arm around my waist and pulled me onto his lap and kissed my head. 'It is only natural that you should feel a little afraid, but Thomas is a good match for you and once you are his wife then love will grow. That is the way of things. Has your mother spoken to you? About the duties of a wife? About what your husband will expect from you?' he asked me, though I sensed that he was uncomfortable, alluding to such personal matters.

I nodded silently. My mother had indeed explained the matters of the marriage bed and I had stared at her in disbelief as she told me what would happen. 'Are you sure?' I had whispered, as my body seemed to freeze and tighten as hard as winter frost at the thought of anyone using me so, let alone Thomas of Lancaster.

'There is pleasure to be found in marriage,' my father told me, although I knew that he and my mother found no such pleasure. 'But you must seek it. You must strive to know Thomas better and to discover what pleases him. He has many attributes. Besides,' he said, 'you made your promise at your betrothal and everything is arranged.'

'But can it not be undone, Papa?' I begged him. 'Truly, I do not want this marriage.'

I heard my voice quiver as it always did when tears threatened, but I made no effort to control my emotion. I knew that once my father saw me cry he would relent. How many times in the past had he sighed and agreed to let me have my way rather than watch my tears.

'I have done it for your wellbeing, my love,' he said seriously, 'and it cannot be changed now. My estates are in the hands of the king and if you do not marry Thomas then I might lose everything. Alicia, this is about more than just your wishes. It is about the future of the de Lacy lands, and your future too. I have done this to safeguard you and you must trust me and be obedient to me in this matter.' When I did not reply he pulled me close against him, although I held myself rigid in his embrace. 'Do not make this hard for yourself — or for me,' he said. 'When the time comes, go willingly to your husband. Be obedient and buxom to him and all will be well, you will see.'

I struggled from his arms and allowed my tears to fall unchecked, still sure that he would relent. But he turned back to his accounts with a sad yet stern face. 'Go now,' he said. 'I have work to attend to here.'

I remained by his side as he moved the tally sticks and took up his quill. But when I saw that he would not change his mind I ran from his presence and up the winding stairs to the bedchamber where I threw myself face down upon my bed and sobbed and sobbed until I ached and shivered as if with fever, and no one who came near offered me any comfort, neither my nurse nor my mother. When I refused to come to dinner they left me hungry. When I said that my head ached my nurse brought me a potion to drink and told me that I had displeased my parents and that I was a wicked girl to make such scenes. And when I protested she reminded me that I was no longer a child to be pampered and cajoled and that I now had obligations to my father and mother that she expected me to fulfil.

'But I hate him!' I cried, speaking of my betrothed. 'And I will never allow him to do those things to me that my mother described. They are too horrible!'

'It is a wife's duty,' said my nurse simply. 'You will only make it worse for yourself if you do not comply.' Then she took the empty cup and left me alone and I tried to comprehend what had changed to make them all so cruel to me when previously I had known nothing but their kindness.

4

Thomas of Lancaster roared with laughter as John de Warenne fell over his outstretched foot and landed face down in the midden.

'You need to learn to look where you're going,' he taunted him as Eble balled his hands into fists and wished that he had the strength and the courage to punch the older boy in his pompous face.

'You tripped him deliberately,' he said.

'You think so do you, Welshboy?' asked Lancaster, sauntering across to where Eble was waiting to unload his own barrow of muck from the stables. He bit back the reply that he was not Welsh, did not come from Wales and that his father was a marcher lord. He had said it all before, but Lancaster had only laughed in his face and told him that his family were so unimportant that he didn't really care where they came from. 'And what do you propose to do about it?' he demanded now.

Eble was filled with the desire to reach out and grasp Lancaster by the hair and force his face into the stinking barrow, but although he knew that he had grown and become stronger

42

during his first year at Pontefract he knew that he was no match for the fifteen year old. Besides he feared a beating if he was found out and he knew that as well as being a bully Thomas was a tell-tale.

Lancaster's face was in his and he drew back. 'Not so brave now then?' he taunted. 'Perhaps you would like to help the fatherless boy finish my work,' he said as he stabbed his pitchfork into the ground perilously close to Eble's foot before calling to his friends amongst the older squires that it was approaching their dinner time.

John was wiping the dung from his face and tunic as best he could. 'One day,' he muttered, 'I will make him regret the way he treats me.'

'Ignore him,' said Eble. 'He will soon be gone.' He knew that he was not the only one who would be glad when the wedding day came and Thomas Lancaster took his bride to Kenilworth Castle and left them in peace. But he felt sorry for the lady Alicia. She was always kind to him and didn't shout at him for standing on her toes during his dancing lessons like some of the other girls. And he was sure that she enjoyed listening to his poems. She would sometimes comment on the things he had written, and say that he had a clever way with words, instead of jeering at him like the older boys did when they caught him scribing his thoughts onto any odd pieces of parchment that he could beg from the clerks.

'I suppose I shall miss my dinner now,' said John.

'Not if we work quickly,' said Eble as he tipped the mess of soiled straw onto the pile and turned the barrow back towards the castle gates. 'Come on. I'll help.'

'Did you know that he is to play the part of King Arthur at the Round Table?' asked John as they began to clear out the stalls of Lancaster's horses.

'Well it is his wedding, so I suppose he has the right,' said Eble, wondering if the lady Alicia would dress as Queen Guinevere. Brides wore their hair loose on their wedding day and he imagined hers hanging freely around her shoulders.

'I thought you were going to help?' said John.

'I am,' replied Eble as he set his mind to the task, knowing that any admiration he had for Alicia could never be anything more than the courtly love that knights had for the ladies whose favours they carried into the tournament. 'I would like to be Sir Lancelot,' he said as he plunged his fork into the stinking straw.

'Sir Miles is to be Lancelot,' said John. 'Besides, we will only serve as squires, holding the horses and picking up the broken lances.'

There was a tone of relief in John's voice. Although a Round Table was a spectacle rather than a hastilude that resembled war, Eble knew that his friend was afraid. He slept on the pallet beside him, just a coffer's width away, and he had heard his nightmares. The other boys just threw anything that was to hand in his direction and told him to shut up, but Eble always tried to say some soothing words as John sat up on his mattress, drenched in sweat and shivering.

'Twas only a dream,' he would tell him, but he knew that the dreams were vivid. He knew that John's father had been killed in the lists, and that his friend believed Thomas of Lancaster's prediction that the same thing would happen to him.

★   ★   ★

As he walked from the clerks' chamber towards the great hall to eat his dinner, Henry de Lacy watched the two figures come running as fast as they could across the bailey. John de Warenne was covered in filth and he wondered what they had been up to.

45

He and Eble le Strange were usually well behaved, but all boys were liable to mischief.

'Send that boy to change his clothing before he comes to table,' he told one of the older squires who was standing near the open doorway. He hoped that the young Warenne wasn't going to become troublesome. His guardian, Robert, Earl of Oxford, had been at his most persuasive when he had asked him to find his grandson a place and in a weak moment, no doubt helped along by the expensive red wine with which Oxford had plied him, Henry had relented. He had felt sorrow for the child. He knew what it was like to grow up without a father and now the boy's mother was dead as well. His own quarrel with the family over some pastureland had been resolved, but a similar disagreement between the Warennes and Alan de le Zouche had resulted in a fight that had left le Zouche mortally wounded. Warenne had been fined and pardoned, but the family of the dead man had not forgiven him. The death of his son, William de Warenne, in the midst of the melee at Croyden just two days before Christmas had been a higher price to pay than the land was ever worth, thought Henry, and a tragedy for young John, who was now slinking off to find a clean tunic.

5

That bright October morning was at odds with my dark mood as my father placed my hand on his and led me across the wide expanse of bailey at Pontefract. He smiled, but I did not think it seemed a genuine smile. He seemed suddenly doubtful and I almost asked him one last time to release me from my promise, but I did not want to make him angry or disappointed in me, or question his wisdom again. He had reassured me that my marriage was a fortunate arrangement, and although I did not agree I had begun to believe that I was wrong in my opinion because I was only a girl and my father was wise and loved me too much to do anything that would bring me harm. Besides, he had delved deep into his coffers to make this marriage a great occasion and fit for the king. The cost of birds for the table alone had been the worth of a small ransom, he said, let alone the wines from France. So I silenced my fears and protests and went with him meekly.

My reluctant hand was placed in the grasp of the bishop of Lincoln, who put it on the damp palm of Thomas of Lancaster. With my free hand I fingered the rubies of the necklace which adorned my neck like drops of blood. It had been given to me as a wedding gift by my grandmother and was the one which she had worn on her own wedding day. Then Thomas pushed a jewelled ring roughly onto my finger. It was done. And my mother, apparently dazzled by the low sun, wiped her eyes on a scrap of linen.

We heard mass and went to a private dinner in the inner chamber. I ate little and my husband did not speak to me but gave all his attention to his cousin Edward, son of the king and heir to the throne of England. With his piercing blue eyes and curling blond hair, he looked a true prince, unlike my dark and swarthy husband.

Soon after noon there was a great fanfare of trumpets and blowing of horns and we went outside to lead the procession to the lists. Beyond the wide open gate I could see the purples and golds of the pennants flapping from the tops of the pavilions that had been erected in readiness for the jousting. Each lady was to lead her mounted knight to the pavilion where his banner flew and from where he would come forth to accept the challenges that had been sent out by letter in the names of the knights of King Arthur and his queen, Guinevere.

I saw Lady de Vescy struggling to keep a grasp on the bridle of the king's horse as it tossed its head. The beast was almost as white as snow and had been brushed until it gleamed from the tips of its pointed ears to the feathers that sprang over its oiled hooves. Under its trapper of embroidered red and gold it stamped first one foreleg and then the other as the king leaned forward to soothe it with gentle words.

My father, still bare-headed, but bearing the de Lacy banner where the rampant lion clawed eagerly at the air, was accepting a token from my mother. She tied the purple and saffron ribbons to the tip of his lance, and when they were secure he bent down and lifted her hand to kiss it to his lips. I hoped that he still loved her and I wished that I had been given the gift of a husband's love.

Thomas offered me his arm and I placed my jewelled hand on his sleeve as we walked to the two ornate chairs which were placed on a berfois, adjacent to the lists. My husband escorted me to one and then seated himself in the other, leaning forward to watch the sport and paying me no attention. I was not disappointed. I thought that my marriage would be easier if he continued to ignore me. Anyway, my eyes were not for him. It was my father I watched as he turned his horse and took up a position facing his opponent, the Earl of Lancaster. The father of the bride against the father of the bridegroom. I felt a frisson of fear. I was afraid that my father would not be victorious, and I needed him to show the king and the Lancasters that the de Lacy blood was not to be bested.

A young squire, Eble le Strange, held his lance as he put on his gilded helm with its purple and yellow plumes. When both men were ready, the herald gave the signal and the knights spurred their horses forward into a ground shaking gallop. I watched my father as he leaned forward in the high-backed saddle. His lance was firmly couched under his arm and he rose slightly in his stirrups as he approached his opponent. I knew that he would have that look of determination that caused a line of three creases to traverse his forehead and I felt my heartbeat quicken as Edmund of Lancaster's lance cracked and shattered against his shield. The crowd cheered and applauded as they finished their run and turned at opposite ends of the lists to recover their breath. Two young squires in the de Lacy livery ran onto the field and quickly and efficiently gathered up the remains of the splintered wood and one of Lancaster's household, bearing his badge of the red rose, handed him a fresh lance.

My palms were slick with moisture as they began their second run. This time my father's aim was true and his lance shattered against the boss of Lancaster's shield. One point each. Then, as the squires took what was left of the broken lance, with my mother's token still attached, and handed him a new one, I saw Lady de Vescy unpin the veil from her jewelled hairnet. She leant over the rail of the berfois and waved it to attract my father's attention. One of the squires said something to him and he began to ride towards her.

'Sir Knight, will you carry my token?' she asked him and with a nod of his head he allowed her to tie the length of flimsy silk to his lance from where it fluttered as he returned to his place. I stared at her and although there was a flush on her cheeks, she did not seem ashamed of what she had done although my mother watched her with a stony face.

My father turned his horse to face Edmund of Lancaster. His horse pawed at the sanded grass and the crowd fell silent in anticipation as the two men eyed one another for a moment from behind the protection of their helms. Then they spurred their horses and I looked left and right as they came on at full tilt. There was a crack of breaking wood and for a moment I was unsure who had struck the winning blow, but as my eyes traced my father down the lists I saw that the broken end of his lance still bore Lady de Vescy's veil. I rose to my feet to applaud him. He was pulling off his helm and below his padded skull cap his face was bright red, but triumphant. He cantered round the lists to the applause of the crowd and as he came full circuit he reined in the destrier and acknowledged me with a bow. I applauded him again, but beside me my husband remained in his seat with a sour face and the moment of pleasure was blighted like a blackfly on his red rose.

*　*　*

The women were singing in the great hall below as my mother and my nurse undressed me as tenderly as if I were yet a child. Many of the men were still drinking in the huge pavilion in the outer bailey and the poor from the town were waiting patiently to see if there were any more scraps from the table. But none of the joy touched me.

I understood, at that moment, the fear of the prisoners as they were dragged up from the dungeon for their execution. I was not held in chains, but I was held by the binding vows I had made before God and man to take

Thomas of Lancaster as my husband. I was not dressed in filthy rags, but in a gown of sky blue which was now being lifted over my head to leave me wearing only the embroidered linen chemise in which I would meet my own fate.

'It will not be so bad as you think,' said my mother gently as she squeezed my hand in hers. 'It seems an unknown thing, but it is only natural and you will find pleasure in it.'

I nodded, not capable of words, and my nurse sent a servant running to tell my husband that I was ready. Too soon there were footsteps on the stairs and men's voices, rendered loud and indiscreet by too much wine and excitement. In the midst of them came Thomas. He too was dressed only in undergarments and his fine shirt of the best Amien linen hung loose over his braies. From the knees down his legs were bare and covered in thick black hair.

Amidst the sounds of shushing, the bishop came forward to say prayers and bless the bed with holy water. The men patted Thomas on the shoulders and wished him good luck, all except for my father who gave him a warning glance and told him to treat me with every courtesy. My lady mother kissed my cheek and one by one they withdrew from the chamber until I was alone with my husband in the candlelight.

'Have you been told what to expect?' he asked.

'Yes, my lord,' I said. I had determined to be meek and not to anger him.

'Lie on the bed then,' he said. 'Let us get it done.'

I turned to the soft mattress with its new sheets and covers of velvet and furs. The striped purple and saffron curtains, embroidered with the de Lacy knot, had been drawn back and I lay down anxiously with my head on the bolster, worried that my chemise was so sheer that Thomas could see my body beneath. He stood looking down at me for a few moments. His eyes travelled from my breasts to my legs and back again, though he showed no sign of liking what he saw. Then he climbed onto the bed and knelt over me and pulled up the linen to uncover me. I grasped the bed covers in both my hands and closed my eyes and prayed to all the saints I could name to preserve me. I flinched as I felt his cold hand on me and I heard myself gasp out loud.

'God's Bones, I barely touched you!' he exploded. 'How am I to consummate this marriage if you do not willingly yield?'

'I am sorry, my lord. I do not mean to

displease you,' I told him as my tears began to flow.

'I would that you were one of the obliging wenches in the tavern below,' he remarked as he roughly pushed my legs apart and lay down between them. The weight of him lying on me made me feel that I could not breathe and I began to gasp in distress.

'Please stop,' I asked him. 'I do not like this!'

'It is not for you to like or dislike it,' he told me. 'I am your husband and it is for you to obey me.'

The pain was more than I had ever endured before and I was certain that I was torn apart by him and must surely die. 'Are you sure that this is right?' I begged. 'It hurts so much it cannot be right and I'm afraid.' I was sure that there was no place inside my body for the huge and rigid member that he forced into me again and again. I could hear his panting breath over the sound of my own sobs and I thought that it would never end. 'Mother of God, help me!' I prayed out loud and my husband groaned and was suddenly still. Then, as he pulled himself from my body, there was another stab of pain and I felt a gush of warm liquid flow from me. He rolled off me and at last I could breathe a little. I reached my fingers to the wet place between my legs and held them up to the candlelight. They were red with blood.

'You must fetch my nurse,' I wept as my body shivered in uncontrollable fits.

Thomas stared down at me with contempt. 'All women bleed the first time. It is nothing,' he replied. 'Be quiet now. If I must sleep beside you I do not want to hear your crying and complaining all night through.' Then he leant to the coffer beside the bed, blew out the candle and pulled the covers around his shoulders. I lay beside him, waiting to die, but at some time in the night as the singing ceased and all grew silent I must have slept for it was morning when I woke again.

When my husband was gone my nurse brought water and cloths to bathe me. She shushed me gently as she wiped away the blood and mess from the insides of my thighs. 'The first time is the worst and you will soon become accustomed to it,' she said as I tried to tell her how much I had suffered.

'I would that I had become a nun,' I told her. 'Why do the minstrels tell stories of love if this is what it means? Surely Guarin de Metz did not do this thing to Mellette. I do not believe that he would hurt her so.'

'Those stories are not about real life. They are to help us forget,' she told me. And I wept again, not just for my pain but for the destruction of my illusion that love was a beautiful thing. No wonder my lady mother denied my father her bed, I thought.

★　★　★

It was not a long journey to the Lancaster's castle at Kenilworth, but with every jolt of the litter I shifted uncomfortably on my cushioned seat. The bleeding had stopped except for a few spots but it hurt me to sit and I wondered if all married women endured such pain.

I saw the countess give me furtive, sympathetic looks from time to time, but she said nothing. We were strangers and I did not want to talk of such matters with her even if she had shown inclination. Our polite exchanges had consisted of no more than her desire that I should be happy and that she wished to know me better, to which I had made appropriate and respectful replies as befitted my new status as her daughter-in-law.

We had fallen into a strained silence, broken only by the creaking of the leather straps and the steady beat of the horses' hooves. My husband was riding ahead of us beside his father. When I lifted the curtain to try to catch sight of where we were I saw his straight back and dark hair as he sat astride a chestnut mare and my stomach contracted in fear of what the coming night would bring.

'It is not far now,' said the countess. Her voice sounded strange after the long silence. 'I know it is hard to leave your home,' she said after a moment and her hand lay briefly on mine. 'Look,' she said, as she lifted the curtain on her own side of the litter. 'You can see the mere if you lean this way a little.' I stared at the wide expanse of water which surrounded the red sandstone walls like a silver mantle. 'My husband says it is where the lady of the lake does dwell,' said the countess.

'The one who guards King Arthur's sword?' I asked, suddenly interested.

'So the earl tells me,' she said with a smile.

I watched the smooth surface as we crossed the long wooden bridge, but I saw no Nimue in the mists with Excalibar in her outstretched hand, and even if she had offered it to my husband I doubt he would have noticed her any more than he would meet my eye as I climbed from the litter and stood wearily in the bailey surrounded by high, yet unfamiliar walls.

My nurse had been allowed to accompany me although I would have no ladies of my own, but would join the countess's household until Thomas and I were of an age to live independently. I was glad of her familiar presence as she helped me wash my hands and face and change my clothing ready for the meal.

'Your cheeks seem pale, my lady,' she observed. 'I hope you do not sicken.'

'I am tired,' I said. 'I wish that I could go to my own bed and sleep undisturbed.'

'That's a fine thing for a bride to want,' she scolded me, 'when there is to be a great feast to welcome you, with dancing and songs.

'I do not want to listen to tales of romance anymore,' I said. 'Not now that the notion is all spoiled.'

'What nonsense you talk,' said my nurse. 'You will come to love your husband when you know him better. That is the way of things. Real love grows slowly. I will go and find the apothecary and beg a little tincture to aid your spirits. An unwilling and sulky wife will not win a husband's heart,' she warned me.

The great hall at Kenilworth was filled with people and the noise of their conversation echoed around the high arched walls. A slight hush fell as Thomas and I were led in by the pipers to take our places at the top table. A chaplain said grace and then the minstrels began to play bright music and the food was borne in on platters carried high in the air by servers and pages. The feast was lavish, as if the Earl of Lancaster wanted to prove that he could present better dishes at table than my father. But I had little appetite and although my husband laid meat upon my platter and offered me his cup to share I partook of little. The songs and vielles of the players seemed out of discord to me and the story that they told of Arthur and Nimue, who held his sword, seemed blemished as my husband laughed out loud.

As I climbed the cold stairs to the bedchamber I could still hear the laughter below and it seemed to mock me. I wept as my nurse undressed me and laid my gown carefully over the wooden pole. The tincture which she stood and watched me drink sent fire around my veins, but the thought of my husband's touch still made me shiver.

'I will sit by the hearth,' I told her when she began to turn back the covers on the bed.

'As you wish, my lady,' she said as she gathered up the cup and my linen for the laundress. 'Try to please him,' she said as she paused by the door. 'You must endeavour to win his love.'

After she was gone I took my cloak from the peg and wrapped it around me to cover the thin chemise. I waited by the fire for him to come, and my heart raced at every sound of approaching footfalls. But they passed by the door and as the castle grew silent, except for the calls of the night watch, I lay down on the bed and with the songs of the minstrels still echoing in my head my thoughts turned to Eble le Strange. He had followed me about at Pontefract like a faithful hound, always eager to do my bidding. When the young squires had come to the chamber in the evenings he had often stood to sing some song that he had written and the ladies had loved him for his sweet voice and clever words. They rewarded him with smiles and the clapping of hands and tasty sweetmeats from a tray on the coffer, although I saw that it was to me he looked to seek approval. And I had always smiled at him for he was a comely boy with his pale hair and his serious expression. But what did he know of love, I wondered, at his young age, except for the lies that he had learnt from the words of others.

At last Thomas came and dropped heavily onto the mattress beside me. He sniffed and coughed a little but did not speak or touch me and he smelt of the cheap perfumes that the prostitutes used. I did not know whether to be sad or happy as I shifted to the very edge of the bed and hugged my arms around myself in a gesture of self-protection.

6

It was the autumn of 1295 and I had been married for a year. I was standing beside the tall narrow windows of the women's chamber at Kenilworth, my head resting against the cold stone, watching as an evening mist gathered around the edges of the mere, hiding any phantoms that might dwell there. I didn't see or hear the messenger, but the Earl of Lancaster came seeking his wife with a worried expression on his face.

'The king has called a parliament at Westminster,' said the earl. 'He wishes to consult with all the principal men to provision for remedies against the dangers which are threatening our kingdom. He asks that we should attend on the Lord's Day next after the feast of St Martin.'

'Then you will need to leave within a day or two,' fussed the countess. 'I must send word to the laundress that your linen must be dried and pressed in readiness.' She hesitated as her mind turned from the essential preparations to more telling concerns. 'Does it mean that you will go to war again,' she said and although she spoke calmly I knew her well enough by now to see that she was troubled by it. 'You are only lately returned from Wales.'

I saw the earl's face cloud with annoyance at his wife's words as if he thought she was issuing him some reprimand, yet I knew that it was his health that concerned her. She had called the apothecary to our chamber twice since her husband's return to discuss what herbs might alleviate the pains that beset his stomach — though when her husband had been given the tincture he had thrown it aside and bid her not to meddle with his wellbeing. It was only later that I saw his temper was rooted in his pain and fear, and that he, like many men, thought that his trouble could be resolved through prayer and abstinence rather than the skills of a physician.

'The messenger tells me that the Scots have made a pact with the French,' he said.

'And Thomas?' she asked. 'Will he go too?'

I waited for the answer to come. If my husband's mother prayed that her son was still too young to go to war then I prayed twice as fervently that he was not.

'Thomas will stay here,' said the earl as he sat down on the bench by the hearth. 'It will do him good to take some responsibility for the running of our English lands whilst I am gone, and you would do well to instruct him.'

I thought that after his father had gone with mine to fight for the king's lands in Gascony that Thomas might change, but left alone, without the guiding hand of either earl, his behaviour worsened.

I was not sorry that he did not come often to my bed or that when he did he was usually too drunk or satiated with the body of another to attempt any coupling with me. But it hurt me deeply when his mother would never acknowledge that her son was anything less than a potential saint. When I sat with her in the women's chamber she would often look me over and ask if there was yet no sign of a grandchild, a son to perpetuate the house of Lancaster. How could I answer? It was not for me to tell her that Thomas abhorred my body. All I could do was shake my head and keep my eyes fixed on my sewing. She would sigh and say that she hoped I would have better news with the next moon. And I felt as if I was judged and found wanting, even though the fault was not my own.

When word came that his father was dead and Thomas now Earl of Lancaster I hoped that his new responsibilities might afford him the opportunity to grow from a rebellious boy into a man, but all that happened is that my husband spent money without restraint and took everything that he wanted — horses, clothes, wines and women. There were always women. I wondered why when I knew that he gave them no pleasure until I saw the rings on their fingers and the necklaces about their necks — jewels that were once mine.

The death of the old earl elevated me to the rank of countess, but did not improve my situation. My husband began to speak of me having a household of my own and I feared that he was planning to send me away. I knew that he would not dare treat me with such contempt whilst my father lived, but in my darkest hours I realised that he would not live forever and that my future without him would be bleak indeed.

There was always war. It went on and on with allegiances changing like the inexplicable patterns of the clouds, and I never questioned why it should be so. No sooner were the Welsh subdued than the Scots rebelled and the French king made battle. English and Norman sailors brawled in the ports. The Welsh and English skirmished amongst themselves when their common enemy was the Scots. And when men weren't fighting they were testing one another in tournaments.

As soon as my father had returned from

France, after arranging the marriage of the young prince, he had come to tell Thomas that he was now old enough to take his part in subjugating the Scots — for they were altogether a more wily people than the Welsh and as soon as one of their leaders was taken from them another appeared. With John Balliol captive in the Tower it had been a brigand by the name of William Wallace who had slaughtered the English at a place named Stirling Bridge and who must now be punished.

My father laid the blame on John de Warenne, not the boy in his household but that boy's grandfather whom he hated anyway. Warenne had thought the matter would be easily solved. Wallace would be captured and put to the sword. He had been so sure, that he had not stirred from his bed until late and had then recalled his men from the far side of the narrow bridge at Stirling and sent a pair of Dominican friars to see if the Scots would come to terms. But Wallace had been determined to do battle and when Warenne had sent his men across the narrow bridge once more he had sent them into the hands of the Scots who thrust their long spears into the horses' sides then pulled men from their saddles and bloodily despatched them to their Maker. Warenne had not crossed the bridge himself and seeing the butchery he had brought about had ordered it destroyed. Leaving only a small body of men to hold the castle against the enemy he had fled south to join the Lord Edward at York. Now it was left to my father and the king to seek redress.

It was the first time Thomas had been to war and on the day that my husband rode out of Bolingbroke Castle, the stronghold where he had taken me to live, to take the road north, I watched from the wall walk. But it was only for my father's safety that I offered prayers. I did not pray that my husband would be killed in battle. That would have been a sin. But neither did I light any candle for his safe return and I would not have grieved had he been returned to me swaddled in waxed linen for burial.

But Thomas and his force of men did return, their banners snapping in the summer wind and the hooves of the weary horses clattering over the deep moat like an echoing drum beat in the hot afternoon air. I had already known from the messengers that they had been successful, that many Scots had been slaughtered where they stood, impaled on the iron tips of English longbows, that they had fallen like blossoms in an orchard when the fruit appears, and I knew that my husband had been knighted on the field of battle.

I watched Thomas rein in his horse in the bailey below me and pull off his helm. He handed it to a squire and I knew that I should go down to greet him and ensure that there was hot water for him to bathe, fresh linen for him to wear and food and drink. That was my duty as a good wife, but as I watched the men and horses filling the bailey I found myself reluctant.

In the end I waited in the great hall until he came to supper, and although Thomas greeted his mother with a kiss he did not even look at me. His forehead still bore the imprint of his chain mail hood and his freshly washed hair was damp as he stood, steaming, before the hearth with a large cup of wine in his hands and boasted of his doings.

'Warenne was of little use again. No wonder his grandson is such an idiot. I don't know why your father ever took him into his household,' he said, suddenly addressing me.

'No, my lord,' I replied, unsure why I should be expected to take any blame for my father's choices. I had always known that there was enmity between the boys and I had felt sorry for young John de Warenne, constantly bullied by the bigger, older squires at the behest of my husband. My father had no good word to say of the elder Warenne either, but he did not abuse the grandson because of it. Once again I measured Thomas of Lancaster against him and found my husband wanting.

7

John de Warenne received the news of his grandfather's death calmly. He did not know the man except by reputation and had often felt embarrassed by the critical talk he heard about his failures in the Scottish wars. The comments stung him in the same way that the laughter and derision of Thomas of Lancaster had hurt him back at Pontefract. His grandfather's shortcomings were not his fault, he knew, but people tended to measure sons and grandsons against their forebears and he thought that people expected him to be little better. His grandfather had failed as a military tactician, his father had failed as a knight and when he heard the scathing talk about their cowardice and incompetence he could not help but wonder if the nightmares that still occasionally beset him held a kernel of truth. Although the Earl of Lincoln had helped him to overcome many of his fears, John still wondered if he would be able to take on the responsibilities that would soon be his.

He watched his friend Eble who was methodically sorting through his baggage and laying to one side all the garments that needed to be mended or cleaned. They had recently arrived back from Aquitaine and were spending some time at the earl's London home to celebrate Christmas.

'You don't have to do that,' he told Eble irritably.

'I don't mind,' he said as he paused with a tunic in his hand. 'And until you have a wife to tell you when to change your dirty underlinen you may as well heed me instead.'

'Perhaps I will find employment for you as my valet after I am wed,' said John. 'I would not be surprised if this summons from the king is to discuss my marriage.'

'And do you have a lady in mind?' asked Eble.

'No,' said John. 'I will have no choice. Whomever the king pleases to give me as a wife I will be obliged to accept. Besides, I have no wish to spend the rest of my life pining for some unattainable lady, like you do for the Countess of Lancaster.' As soon as he had spoken John regretted his words. He wished that he could clasp a fist around them and dash them to the ground unheard, but it was too late. Eble kept his gaze fixed on the clothing that he was spreading across the trestle table and, although his back was turned, John knew that he had wounded him unintentionally. His friend's regard for their lord's daughter had neither faltered nor lessened in the years since her marriage and he should have known better than to remark on it in jest. 'At least you will be able to take a wife of your own choosing,' he added lamely by way of an apology.

'I am not much to be desired,' said Eble with a shrug of his shoulders. 'What can a younger son with no estates offer? The earl has spoken of me becoming a clerk or even taking orders and I have thought on it.'

'You? A monk?' laughed John. 'Oh you would look fine with a tonsured head,' he said, trying to imagine a bald pate poking up through his friend's thick fair hair. 'They whip themselves, you know, to stop their lustful cravings.'

Eble gathered up the soiled clothing for the laundress and turned from the table, his task finished. 'It is the rising in the night to pray that I would find the hardest,' he admitted.

'The rising in the night is exactly the problem I refer to,' laughed John and ducked as Eble threw a pair of braies at his head. 'No. You must be my squire and I will find you a willing wife,' he told him, thinking that it was time his friend stopped comparing all women with the countess and finding that they fell short of his ideal. Courtly love and romance was a thing for women and untried boys, he thought, and it was time that Eble grew up and discovered what a real woman could do for him.

★ ★ ★

When John eventually attended on the king in his private chamber on a snowy morning he was surprised to be told that he was to live on his estates at Guildford.

'We will hold a tournament there to celebrate,' said Edward.

John looked up from where he was kneeling and saw the glint of challenge in the king's eyes. So, he thought, it is to be a test to ascertain that I am not still too fearful to ride the lists.

'It would be a great honour, sire, especially if you were to attend.'

'I think I will come,' said the king. 'And I will bring the queen to watch you. She is much your age and will enjoy the sport.'

'Yes, sire,' agreed John, wondering how the young Queen Marguerite felt about being wedded to such a white haired old man — although she had given him two more sons and rumour was that her belly was swelling with a third.

'I will bring the Lord Edward too, and the

Earl of Lancaster. Let us see how you fare against him,' said the king, rubbing his hands together in anticipation of the sport.

'I look forward to it, sire,' said John, his stomach turning at the thought of facing Thomas of Lancaster in a joust.

The bad weather meant that the tournament was delayed and every day that passed was an agony of waiting. It angered John because he knew that he could have been enjoying the freedom of being the lord over his own lands if it hadn't been for the nagging worry of the joust. And it was not as if he was untried. There had been many such tournaments in Aquitaine, but fighting a Frenchman seemed tame in comparison with what was to come. He knew that he would be judged on his performance. Judged by his grandfather's old enemies and by the king as to whether he was worthy to be given his inheritance, a knighthood, and a wife.

He wished that he had Eble to talk to. But his friend remained in the service of the Earl of Lincoln and John's suggestion that he might accompany him as a squire had been refused with a quick ferocity that had surprised him. John missed Eble more than he had expected. They had been close in one another's company for so many years that it was odd not to walk into the hall at dinnertime and be able to tell his friend about some incident that had occurred during the morning. He missed being able to confide in Eble whom he knew saw his weaknesses and yet did not think less of him for them.

At length the ice thawed enough for the knights and squires of many households to begin arriving at Guildford, and those who could not be found beds within the manor house put up their tents and pavilions in the shelter of the wall that surrounded the bailey. John greeted them all courteously, outwardly confident in his new status but inwardly quaking and every hour seeking only the sight of the purple and saffron colours of the Earl of Lincoln which would mean that he could be re-united for a time at least with Eble.

John woke, sweating, from a nightmare that had seen him unhorsed and bleeding to death. A lance had cut straight through his mail like a blacksmith's hot iron. The dream had been so vivid that his hand was clutched to his side to stem the imaginary flow of blood. But as he regained his senses and sat up in the curtained bed, wishing for the comfort of his friend's arm around his shoulders, he realised that he was unharmed and that it was yet early. No one else stirred and he could not yet hear the morning sounds that told him it was time to get up.

He lay back on his bolster and stared at the darkness. He did not want to sleep again for fear of more bad dreams although he knew that tiredness would not help him to do his best in the trial that was to come. He tried to comfort himself by remembering the words that the Earl of Lincoln had spoken to him before he retired to bed.

'I have seen you joust,' he had said. 'And I know that you can beat Thomas easily if only you put your fears and doubts aside. Have courage.' And he had patted him on the shoulder in a gesture that had meant much to him. He liked and admired the earl who had been more of a father to him than any member of his own family and he wished to please him, even if that pleasure could only be achieved with the defeat of the man's son-in-law.

At length the night that crept around the edges of the shutters faded to a dark grey and one of his Guildford servants came with water for John to wash before he went to hear mass. He had never prayed so hard for his soul as he did that cold morning as he shivered on his knees before his chaplain. The small chapel was crowded with visitors and their breath hung in clouds on the cold air as the deep voices of both his friends and enemies repeated a heartfelt amen and got up, rubbing at sore knees and stiff backs, to file through the narrow doorway and into the hall where smoking braziers were warming the morning air and the breakfast was laid out on the trestles.

A trickle of sunlight found its way through a window and promised a fine day to come. It would not be long now, thought John, as he shook his head at the boy who was placing bread and cheese on his platter. His stomach was too filled with turmoil for him to be able to eat. He took a sip of the weak ale and looked around the room. Thomas of Lancaster was laughing loudly and he stared at John with a derisive expression on his dark face and made some whispered comment to his companion.

'He plays games with your mind,' said the Earl of Lincoln who had sat down beside him. 'Do not allow him to win before you are even horsed. Perhaps you would like Eble le Strange to assist you to arm?' he suggested.

John was more grateful than he could express for the offer and as Eble lifted the heavy mail shirt over his head and pulled it straight he wanted to tell his friend how glad he was to have his company.

'It's like old times,' he said.

'You make it sound as if we have been

parted for years,' remarked Eble as he smoothed the tunic that bore John's arms of blue and gold checks over the closely riveted metal rings.

'Have you not missed me?' asked John in a tone that he hope would be taken for jest.

'Like a pain in the arse,' replied Eble with a grin.

The hall had grown warm and when they stepped outside John felt his breath taken away by the cold air. There was, as yet, no sign of springtime on the branches of the bare trees where the hoar frost still lingered and the ground underfoot was as hard as iron. Eble held the reins of his black destrier as he put a foot to the stirrup and mounted feeling trepidation as well as his armour weighing him down.

'For all our sakes,' said Eble as he handed him first his chequered shield and then his lance, 'knock the smug look from his face.'

'I'll do my best,' promised John from within the confines of his helm. He could see only a narrow portion of the field but could feel the eyes of the spectators on him and his opponent as he turned his horse to face his worst nightmare. He tightened his fingers around the lance and backed the horse a few paces to steady it. The animal shook its head and John knew that it resented the confines of the protection over its face and ears. It stamped a hoof in impatience and John mentally crossed himself as he focused on the Earl of Lancaster who waited beside a squire who held aloft a banner on which fluttered the badge of a red rose.

Lancaster's shield was decorated with three golden lions and, with a prayer to St George to assist him in slaying every one as if they were dragons, John touched his spurs to his horse's flanks and heard the cold wind whistle as it was forced through the slits in his helm, making his eyes water and almost blinding him. As his horse settled into its stride below him, he shifted the lance slightly with his heavily gloved fingers and gritted his teeth as he kept his eyes fixed on the red and gold shield, intent on making a central strike. But before he knew what had happened his opponent was out of sight and John cursed at himself for missing. He pulled hard on the reins and a squire ran forward to stop the excited horse before they galloped on, out of the lists and down to the frozen beck beyond. He turned and blinked hard to clear his vision. Lancaster was also lining up for the second run and this time John was determined to strike the first blow. Swallowing blood from biting his tongue he secured the lance under his arm and nodded briefly to the squire who stepped back. The herald lowered the flag and, as the hooves below him pounded the solid ground, he kept his eyes on the approaching shield, remembering the Earl of Lincoln's lesson that you strike the place you are looking at. This time he saw Lancaster veer away from him at the last moment and tried to compensate. He felt the shock of impact judder down his arm to his shoulder as he momentarily swayed in the saddle, only the raised cantle preventing him from falling backwards. At the far end of the lists it was Eble who caught his horse.

'You almost had him,' he said as John turned the destrier in a tight circle. 'He has a habit of ducking slightly and pulling his horse to the right. Aim lower and further to his inside,' he advised as he passed John a strip of linen cloth to wipe his eyes. John nodded, adjusted his helm and readied himself for the final run. He would not be bested by Lancaster on his own land, he decided. The man underestimated him and was playing with him. He would see now that the time for games was over. He settled his weight evenly in the saddle and muttered a few encouraging words to the horse. He saw Eble pat its heaving flanks and step back, the wind blowing his hair across his face.

'God be with you,' he heard him say as he

spurred the horse. This time he took his aim off centre as his friend had advised and, as Lancaster twisted to avoid him and strike a blow of his own, John did not allow his mount to break stride but thrust his lance towards the head of the middle lion. The pain in his shoulder was enough to reassure him that the strike was true. From around him came a roar of voices and he saw that his lance was broken. As the squire grabbed for his reins he dropped what remained of his weapon to the ground and pulled off his helm for a better look. Thomas of Lancaster was lying on the frozen ground gasping for his breath like a landed fish and the crowd was applauding. John knew that his enemy would hate him even more from now on, but for the moment he did not care. He paused and bowed in his saddle to the king, to the young queen wrapped in furs beside him and to the Earl of Lincoln who stood to acknowledge him with a proud smile.

'Well done,' he mouthed over the uproar and John allowed himself to grin with satisfaction as he returned with Eble to his pavilion to disarm. He hoped that he had done enough to be given his inheritance and he vowed that Thomas of Lancaster would never again be allowed to set foot on any land that he owned.

Henry de Lacy found that his face was aching both from the cold and the smile that followed John de Warenne as he left the lists in triumph. Was it a bad thing, he wondered, to feel so pleased at the sight of his son-in-law being helped up from the ground, angrily waving his men away yet unable to stand without their assistance. What would Alicia have made of it, he wondered, disappointed that she had not come and scarcely believing Thomas's excuse that she had pleaded to be excused as the winter was so cold. Even if she was with child, as he hoped she was, he was sure that she would have wanted to come and there had been no such pleading from the young queen who looked radiant as she sat snugly wrapped and glowing with the quickening of a third baby.

'I'll let the lad stay if he sends me some barrels of salted deer,' remarked Edward as he watched John leave the field. 'He's done well. What do you think of a match between him and my granddaughter, Jeanne?'

'She is still young. Not yet ten years old,' said Henry.

'A young woman is just the thing for a man,' laughed Edward, reaching to pinch Marguerite's cheek. 'Look how she blushes. Is she not a prize?' he asked and Henry saw that despite his initial reluctance to go through with the marriage the king seemed genuinely fond of his French wife.

'Indeed. But your granddaughter will not be able to give Warenne sons just yet,' Henry reminded him, 'and patience is a virtue rarely found in young men.'

8

Eble wasn't sure how to react to the news. Both his brothers had been chosen to be among the company of over two hundred men to be knighted alongside the Lord Edward, but he had not. He sat moodily on the top of a barrel in the storeroom at the Earl of Lincoln's London house, kicking his heels against the strips of wood and enjoying the way that the sound echoed from its empty depths. Was it sulking to ponder on something that seemed unfair, he wondered. Such a lot of things that happened seemed unfair.

Since John de Warenne had gone to his estates at Guildford he missed him more than he had ever thought possible, yet he still felt an unwelcome sense of jealousy that his friend was to become Sir John, whilst he remained a mere squire. The Earl of Lincoln had patted him on the shoulder and told him not to fear, that his turn would come, but it was small comfort. He had heard that the Countess of Lancaster would be in attendance and he would have dearly loved to kneel and receive his belt, sword and spurs knowing that she was watching him.

Alicia. She had been married for ten years now and still he thought about her every day. His friends had long since given up trying to persuade him to visit the stews with them and he knew that it was common talk that his friendship with John de Warenne included a relationship that was sexual in nature and that it was for him that Eble pined and wrote his poetry.

'Is your work done?' The irritated voice of the earl made him jump guiltily down from his perch and pull his tunic straight.

'Everything is ready, my lord,' he reassured him. 'I have sent the boys for their dinner.'

'And are you not hungry?'

'I was on my way, my lord.' Eble watched the frown crease the earl's forehead. He often had the impression that he was a disappointment to him, but he wasn't sure what to do to rectify it. He performed his work to the best of his ability and was conscientious in every task. Even now, as the earl glanced around he could find nothing that was not attended to.

'Very well. Go and eat,' he told him. 'Have you seen your father and your brothers?'

'Not yet, my lord.'

'Seek them out after your dinner. I have no more need of you here for a few days and your place is with your family for this important event.'

'Yes, my lord. Thank you,' replied Eble, knowing that if he went looking for anyone it would be John.

The London streets were crowded with all the men and their retinues and families who had come for the celebration. Around Westminster carpenters had constructed temporary buildings on any scrap of ground that could be found and at the New Temple walls had been levelled and fruit trees cut down to make space for the hundreds of tents and pavilions that were required for the robing and knighting of so many men.

Eble made his way to the church of the Knights Templar where those who were to be knighted were housed and where they were to spend the night in silent vigil, though judging from the uproar that was already coming from within as he approached the door he could not imagine that much silence would be kept during the dark hours to come. He squeezed through the crush of excited men, his eyes gradually accustoming themselves to the gloom after the bright sunshine outside and his nostrils to the pervading aroma of sweaty bodies.

It was impossible to see further than the men who surrounded him, pushing and jostling with sharp elbows and heavy feet, unaware and uncaring of his attempts to part a way through the crowd. Mostly he was ignored and the few people he did ask shrugged their shoulders in response to his enquiries about John de Warenne. Then, as if he had been led there by more than chance, he saw the familiar blue and gold of the Warenne colours near to the prone effigy of William Marshal, and he determinedly elbowed his way towards his friend.

'What? Shirking your duties again?' John greeted him with a wide smile and a cuff around the ear.

'I am seeking my family, but they seem to be as hard to find as frost on a May morning.'

'I saw your father earlier. I think they have pitched their tents outside.'

'I will go and search for them there then,' he said.

'Don't go just yet,' said John, reaching out a hand towards him. 'Stay and talk with me awhile. I wanted to ask if you would attend my wedding,' he went on. 'It's to be in three days' time. I would like you to be there.'

'It will be odd to see you wed,' said Eble, unable to prevent himself from brushing some dust from the tunic that hung on a pole ready for John to wear on the morrow.

His friend shrugged. 'I have only met the girl a couple of times. She's barely more than a child, but they assure me she will grow. I shan't bed her for a while yet,' he said. 'So it will not make much difference to me. She will come to live in my household, but she has her own servants and I doubt I'll see much of her.'

'Is it what you want?' asked Eble sitting down on the closed lid of John's travelling coffer and looking up at his friend. John had grown into a comely man, well-proportioned and tall, and Eble saw that his light brown hair and beard had both been recently trimmed. Women found him attractive and Eble had seen many whose eyes followed him as he strode confidently along.

'She is the king's granddaughter. 'Tis an honour,' he said. 'And do not think to lecture me on love again,' he warned with a glint in his grey eyes.

Eble spread his hands in a gesture of defeat. 'But do not say you were not warned when, one of these days, you fall in love.'

John folded his arms and grinned down at him. 'But you will come to my wedding?'

'I'll come,' agreed Eble. 'The earl has given me some leave to be with my family — which means that I had better go and seek them out.'

Henry de Lacy felt joy rush through him at the sight of his daughter as she hurried across the hall of his London house to greet him. Pulling her up from her curtsey he gathered her into his arms and kissed the top of her head through the expensive silk veil, but as he ran a hand down her back he felt the bones of her spine and he released her from his tight embrace as he suddenly became aware of her fragility.

'Are you well?' he asked as he studied her pale face. The pretty girl he had given away in marriage to the king's nephew was gone and in her place stood a woman who was a mere shadow of the Alicia that he loved.

'I am well, father,' she replied after a momentary hesitation and he was relieved to see the gleam of pleasure in her dark eyes as she looked up at him. He wondered if she was with child. He knew that many women suffered sickness in the early months and sometimes grew thin before their bodies rounded with new life. He longed to ask, but knew that she would confide in her mother first.

'Your mother is resting,' he said. 'The journey tired her, but I will send word that you are here.'

'No,' said Alicia with a hand on his sleeve. 'Let her rest. I am content with you for the time being.'

Henry drew his daughter towards the hearth. Even though it was May there was yet a chill in the air and he did not want her to catch cold. It was a full ten years since she had wed Thomas of Lancaster and each year he had hoped for news of a grandson to continue the de Lacy line. He had heard, to his anger, that Lancaster had sired a son on some woman in his household, but Alicia remained childless and he wondered if her husband was neglecting her.

'Does your husband treat you well?' was all he ever inquired and his daughter's brief nod and the way that she quickly began to speak of other things often told him that his fears were probably true. He regretted what he had done but could see no way to undo it.

'Where is everyone?' she asked, taking in the almost deserted house.

'I have given most of them leave. Many have family who have come to London and others are amongst those who are to be knighted.'

'Eble le Strange?' asked Alicia.

'No. His brothers have been chosen but not him. He is a little put out,' remarked Henry with a slight smile, 'but I have been making inquiries for a more fitting position for him than that of knighthood. I think he would do well in orders.'

'Eble?' she said and he hesitated at her surprise.

'Do you not agree?'

'I cannot see him as a monk or priest,' she replied. 'Does he not wish to take a wife?'

'He has shown no inclination. His friendships seem to be confined to men.' Henry hesitated, unsure how to explain his suspicions to his daughter. Alicia snorted with laughter.

'If you think his carnal inclinations are towards his own sex then you are shorter sighted than I took you for,' she scolded him. 'He may not be promiscuous but I can assure you that it is the love of women that interests him.'

Alicia stayed to dine with them and spent some time with her mother before going home as twilight began to edge across the clear sky. Henry himself escorted her back to her husband's house and kissed her goodnight, reluctant to part with her.

He rode home by way of the Abbey Church where a chosen few of the men were keeping a silent vigil with the young prince. They were all to receive their knighthoods tomorrow, Whit Sunday. More still were keeping vigil in the Temple Church, though the atmosphere across the city was one of excited anticipation rather than reverential silence. Henry sighed. This generation of young men who were gathered in London were the future of the country. On their shoulders would rest the responsibilities for ensuring that England remained a powerful and prosperous land. He was growing older, as was the king. Edward had only recently recovered from illness and Henry suspected that it was the prospect of his demise that had prompted him to ensure that his son was knighted. Although the queen had presented Edward with another daughter he was fast approaching his life span of three score years and ten. Neither of them would live forever no matter how much they wished it.

★   ★   ★

Henry watched the next morning as the prince knelt before his father in the private chapel at the Palace of Westminster. The king's hand trembled as he touched his sword to his son's shoulders before fastening the belt of knighthood around him. Henry stepped forward, along with the Earl of Hereford, and fastened golden spurs to young Edward's feet. All the while the young prince remained solemn and Henry could not decide if it was because he was overawed at the ceremony or because he and his father had had another quarrel.

When the ceremony was done they made their way to the Abbey where the other candidates were to be knighted. Outside it was reminiscent of a melee, with ungoverned noise and chaos filling the streets. Men-at-arms on destriers were holding back the pressing crowds and clearing a path for those who were to enter the precincts of the church. Everywhere there seemed to be laughing and shouting and trumpet calls as the men in their fine new clothes walked in the sunshine to the Abbey. At length those who should be inside were ushered in and those who had no business there were kept firmly out. The great doors were closed with a resounding thud that quieted the gathered congregation and the prince took his place before the high altar where he knighted the men, who were called forward in pairs.

Henry watched as they knelt before the prince. Tall men, smaller men. Dark haired and fair. Most were young and virile though there were some older men such as Roger Mortimer of Chirk who had reached middle age without ever being knighted. He wondered how long it would be before the tall young man wielding his sword before the altar was kneeling there to be anointed as their king — and if he would live to see it. Prince Edward did not have his father's appetite for war, but that did not mean he would be a bad king, thought Henry. Sometimes young men changed when they were allowed to step out of their father's shadow and he hoped that it would be the case with him.

Henry smiled as John de Warenne came forward, paired with Hugh le Despenser. Both were to be married to granddaughters of the king within a few days. These would be the men, along with his son-in-law Thomas, who would serve young Edward as he served the present king. Henry prayed that God would guide them in their futures, and he felt a pang of regret that his own sons could not have been a part of this great day.

There followed a huge feast in the Great Hall of Westminster Palace. The king had raided his coffers to present a lavish occasion and the famished knights attacked their food with all the vigour of a quest. Once the first urgent pangs of hunger had been assuaged two swans were born in by musicians and the king called on all those knights present to take a vow on the swans to avenge the injuries done by Robert Bruce who had murdered his rival John Comyn before the altar of a Scottish priory and had himself crowned king of Scotland. The men cheered and held up their cups and stamped their feet and vowed that they would fight. And Prince Edward vowed that he would not sleep in the same place twice until he reached Scotland.

★ ★ ★

'I have told the prince to heed you well,' the king told Henry as they watched the tournament that followed the next day. 'Watch him well and tell me how he fares,' he said as they discussed the tactics that should be used against the Scots. 'If I had not been so sure of the Queen Eleanor I would question whether he is any son of mine, he is so different from what I would expect my flesh and blood to be. It's a shame that Alfonso died when he did. That boy had the makings of a warrior and a valiant knight. This boy,' he said, 'seems only interested in rowing boats and digging ditches. Not even his companion Piers Gaveston seems able to make a man of him.'

'He is yet young, sire,' said Henry, surprised at the open contempt with which the king spoke of his son. 'He will come round. You will see.'

Henry winced as the bright sun glinted off a shield and reflected into his eyes. The wine at the feast had been good and strong and in the excitement of the day he had drunk more than was wise. Though not as much as some of the knights who looked as if they had woken with very sore heads that morning to the news that the king had been in earnest and meant to hold them to their vows to fight the Scots.

9

I could not help but smile at the sight of the excited girl who was hopping from one foot to the other as she stood beside Sir John de Warenne, her new husband. Although it made me feel suddenly old. It seemed only a summer or two since John had come to join my father's household at Pontefract as a small shy boy and now here he was, grown and knighted and wed to the king's granddaughter. Little Jeanne, in her blue dress and with her long flowing hair crowned with a chaplet of bright flowers was looking up at her husband adoringly as she clung to his hand. He merely looked uncomfortable. It was clear that he felt no physical attraction towards her, but that was a good thing. She was far too young for the marriage bed and hopefully love would grow as they came to know one another until such time as they consummated their marriage in mutual desire and respect.

'My lady,' said John as he bowed to me when I went forward to kiss the bride.

'I was going to bid you to be a good husband to your wife,' I said, 'but I am sure you have heard enough such advice for today.'

'I am sure it cannot be repeated too often, my lady,' he replied courteously. 'And I shall heed your words.'

'She is very young,' I said as I took a strand of Jeanne's silky hair in my fingers. The way that she was watching her husband suddenly reminded me of the dog that Thomas had had at Pontefract, the one which he had whipped for tripping him in the stable. 'Do not hurt her,' I said, meeting John's eyes to ensure that he understood my meaning. He looked momentarily affronted then shook his head.

'Have no fear, my lady. I have no intention . . . '

'Indeed,' I said, laying a hand on his sleeve. 'Forgive me. I was presumptuous.'

He nodded and I moved away to where my father was speaking with Isabella de Vescy. They fell silent as I approached them.

'Where is my lady mother?' I asked.

'She has gone inside to rest,' said my father and I sensed an awkwardness about him that was unusual. I wondered if it was because he was reminded of my own wedding and if he regretted not listening to my pleading to be released from my promise.

'I will go to her,' I said and went from the spring sunshine into the gloomy interiors where at last I found my mother lying down on a bed, surrounded by anxious waiting women. She looked pale and I knelt beside her and took her hand in mine. 'Are you unwell?' I asked.

'I felt a little faint,' she whispered. 'There is no need for fuss.' But as I looked at her I could see that she had grown thin and that her face was etched with the frowns that constant pain had wrought there.

'What does the physician say?'

'He examines my urine, he bleeds me and then goes away leaving only ghastly tinctures for me to drink. Alicia,' she said, struggling to sit up, 'I am afraid. I think God's punishment is upon me.'

I stared at her bluish lips in silence for a moment, not knowing how to reply. 'What makes you say such a thing?'

She waved at the women to leave us and pulled me closer. 'Alicia. I have sinned and been a bad wife to your father. I have refused him and given him no more sons to replace the ones that were taken from us.' She began to cry and I did not know how to comfort her. It was unlike my mother to confide in me. 'I have denied him the marriage bed and because I have refused to bear him more children the devil has come to inhabit my womb instead. Something grows there, Alicia. I can feel its weight and I am afraid that I will be forced to give birth to a demon.'

She shook with sobs of anguish and fear and I took her in my arms as if she were a child and gave her what comfort I could. 'Hush, hush,' I soothed as I rocked her gently to and fro. 'No one ever gave birth to a demon in this life. You have listened to too many stories.'

After a while she calmed and when she had wiped her eyes and withdrawn from my embrace to lie back on her pillows she reached out a hand to touch my cheek. 'And what of you, Alicia. Will you give me a grandson before I die?'

'If it is God's will, Mama,' I told her.

But I knew that it was not what God, or my husband, willed for me. Thomas's coldness towards me was deliberate. He knew well enough the terms of our marriage contract; he knew that my lands would remain in his possession if I bore him no children. It made me fearful. If I gave him no son then I was better to him dead than alive. And even though my body was repulsed by him it craved children. Every time one of my ladies wed and bore a child I was plunged a little deeper into my personal sadness. They would come to me with the love and satisfaction of motherhood shining from their eyes and a small swaddled bundle would be placed in my arms. And as the babes lay there, their heads heavy in the crook of my elbow and their baby scent clinging on the air, they were all Margaret. How many had I carried to the chapel to be baptised? For how many had I stood before the priest and made vows to God to watch over them and protect them from Satan and all his works? How many little girls running through the chambers of northern castles have the name Alicia? And not one of them is mine. Not one is the flesh wrought from my own flesh, and whilst my husband continued to despise and abhor my body I knew that I would never again hold a baby that carried the de Lacy blood.

I had seen the disappointment in my father's eyes when he felt the emptiness of my body in his arms. I felt as if I had failed him by not providing the grandson which would carry his blood if not his name into the next generation. I knew that his surrender of his lands first to the king and then to my husband had been a gamble that he had thought to win. My father was not normally a risk taker, but surely he should have known from the loss of both my brothers that heirs are often a rare commodity.

I knew that my husband had a mistress, more than one, and that he had given two sons to other women. Sons that should have been mine. And I grew to hate him for his contempt of me.

I was not sorry when he left me and rode for Scotland. Although I hardly saw him and he rarely spoke more than the odd word to me, the oppression of his presence lifted as the thunder clouds rolled away on that June afternoon. A happier atmosphere pervaded the castle when he was not there.

I had been glad to leave London. The brutal execution of William Wallace had sickened me as much as it had delighted my husband and when I had heard him laughing at table as he described the man's agony I wondered if he was quite sane, but knew better than to voice any opinion. If my husband did pay me any attention it always ended painfully in some way or another and I learnt early in our marriage to say nothing even if such willing subjugation was against my nature.

10

Henry hurried along the passageway and down the twisting steps. The young page boy ran ahead of him, glancing back at every turn as if to urge him on faster.

'This way, my lord,' he kept repeating as if Henry were a stranger to the palace.

The king's voice, raised to its fullest limit, bounced off the walls and out of the part open door. 'You want to give away lands?' he raged. 'You, who have never earned any? As God lives, if it was not for the fear of breaking up the kingdom I would never let you enjoy your inheritance!'

William Langton, who had sent the boy to fetch him, was peering fearfully through the gap and turned with a look of relief as Henry approached. Pushing past him, Henry was just in time to see the king give his son one last kick as he lay prostrate amongst the floor rushes. By the time he reached Edward to restrain him the king had slumped down onto a bench. He was trembling, though whether it was with rage or fatigue Henry could not be sure.

Henry watched as the king brushed away

the blond hairs that he had torn from his son's head and, with a look of disgust on his face, called for water and a towel to wash his hands. The Lord Edward was pulling himself slowly to his feet with wary eyes on his father and Henry gestured to him that he should leave. 'I will attend to the king,' he told him quietly, and as the prince limped away, Henry wondered what he had done to cause such outrage.

The king was slowly recovering his breath and Henry gestured for the page boy to bring wine. Edward gulped it down and wiped his mouth.

'That boy will be the death of me. And God knows what will happen then,' he said, his voice quavering as he spoke.

Henry's eyes met those of William Langton, who had followed him into the chamber. He raised one eyebrow.

'The Lord Edward sent me to the king to beg licence to promote Piers Gaveston to the rank of the Count of Ponthieu,' he explained.

Henry felt both his eyebrows rise in sharp surprise.

'The boy did not even have the courage to come and ask himself!' spat the king. Revived by the wine he flung the empty cup into the hearth. 'Why is that do you think?' he demanded. Henry tactfully shook his head, though he knew the reason was that the prince was afraid of his father. It was at times such as these that the Lord Edward missed a mother to intervene on his behalf and Henry thanked God that his own mother was still spared to continue to give him the benefit of her wisdom.

'Gaveston will have to go,' said the king. 'I shall send him back to Gascony. The prince has too many companions in his household anyway.' He waved them away and called for the page to assist him to the privy. As they bowed from the chamber Henry turned to William Langton to express his concerns, but it was Langton who spoke first as he drew him aside into a quiet alcove.

'I think it is for the best that the king sends Piers Gaveston away,' he said. 'Did you know that he and my lord, the prince, have sworn to be brothers-in-arms? They have even performed the ceremony,' he went on. 'They have mingled their blood in a vessel and received the host side by side. That is why the prince wants Gaveston to share his inheritance.'

Henry stared at the man. Swearing to be brothers-in-arms was an old chivalric tradition that dated from the legends of King Arthur. Men swore to fight side by side and protect one another in all battles and quarrels and to have the same friends and enemies.

'I think you may be taking this too seriously,' said Henry after a moment. 'Many young men swear such bonds, but it is chivalry and play, nothing more.'

The treasurer shrugged and Henry patted him on the shoulder and told him not to fret, but he knew that neither of them had heard the last of it and he was not surprised when a distraught Lord Edward sought him out and asked for his advice.

'If I can just keep Piers and Gilbert de Clare,' he pleaded. 'It is more than I can bear to be separated from my friends. My father will not listen. What should I do?'

Although the prince was a grown man now, Henry thought that he was about to break down and weep his anguish was so raw.

'I think that it might be for the best to comply with your father's wishes,' he advised him. 'In time he may soften and allow your friends to be recalled. And he is allowing Gaveston to remain until after the next joust so it is not as if you are to be parted from him immediately. We all have to learn to spend time away from those we love,' he told him, thinking not of the prince but of his own longing to see Bella again.

But the king refused to relent. Although he agreed to pay Gaveston a yearly pension of a hundred marks he told him that he must return to his home in Gascony and remain there. The Lord Edward was inconsolable and in the end his father agreed that he could accompany Piers to Dover to see him onto his ship rather than joining the army on campaign in Scotland.

Henry was not sorry that Edward and his son were apart. The row had done neither of them any good and the king seemed worn out by it. With the passing of each day he seemed to be diminishing in size and strength and it reminded Henry of the way that Edmund had died in France. He knew that the king was ill and that he was visiting his privy more and more often because of the flux, but Edward would never admit that there was a problem and he continued with his plans to wage war once more on the Scots.

★ ★ ★

'Sire, I do not think you are well enough to go on,' said Henry. The king was lying on a bed in the infirmary of Lanercost Priory and Henry doubted that he could stand, still less mount a horse and lead an army. Their progress north had been slow and tortuous as the king's recurrent illness had forced them to stop and rest many times, either in the castles of his subjects or in local abbeys and priories where the medical expertise of the monks seemed to be achieving little in the way of a cure.

'I am well enough,' he argued. 'And no one else seems capable of completing the task, so what choice do I have but to go on myself?' Sweat broke across his brow with the effort of his words and a silent monk gently wiped the king's face with a strip of scented linen. 'I will not be satisfied until I have shown Robert Bruce that he cannot prevail against me, and I will continue to punish those who assist him to defy me.'

Henry wondered if these wars with the Scots would ever end. Edward had been firm to the point of cruelty with Bruce's supporters and even his little daughter Marjorie would be now swinging in a cage from the turret of one of his castles if Henry had not intervened on her behalf and persuaded Edward to send her to a convent instead. But nothing appeared able to stop the Scot and the stories that were being whispered alarmed him.

★   ★   ★

By July, the summer had shone its face for only a few days and the weather had settled into a cold and wet pattern that showed no sign of changing. The army had finally reached Burgh-on-Sands on the English side of the Solway Firth and made camp. Staring through the gloom, Henry could see Scotland across the brownish rolling waters. The king had told him that as soon as he had gathered his strength they would march across the border and defeat Bruce for once and all. But Henry doubted that the king would be fit to travel further for many days yet. His servants had put him to bed in his tent and his physician had attended him, but left with a grave look on his face. It was a look that Henry had seen before; one which betrayed that there was no hope and that it was only a matter of time.

When a breathless messenger arrived at his tent at dinner time the next day he assumed that the king had worsened.

'My lord, you must come right away,' said the man with a stricken look.

Henry picked up a cloak to cover his mail shirt from the persistent drizzle and walked across the oozing mud towards the king's tent. Inside, the scent of bruised grass which accompanied them everywhere was overpowered by the sickening stench of human excreta, but it was the alarming silence that made Henry's heart pound in fear. The men of the king's bedchamber were standing around the travelling bed. Not one lifted his eyes as he approached, and even before he saw the body Henry knew that the king was dead.

'We came to get him up to eat his dinner,' whispered one after a moment. 'He died in our arms.'

Henry made the sign of the cross and one by one the men knelt to pray for the king's soul. It was the moment Henry had been dreading. He knew that now everything would change.

Henry needed a fast and reliable messenger to take word to the Lord Edward that he was now king. He needed someone who could be discreet and tactful and ensure that the young king heard the news from Henry's own letter and not from some rumour that had been spilled along with too much beer in an inn along the way.

'Find Eble le Strange and tell him to come to my tent at once,' he ordered. 'And bring me some parchment and quills.'

'Shall I bring a clerk as well, my lord?'

'No, just Eble le Strange,' repeated Henry. 'And have the four fastest horses we own saddled and ready to leave within the hour.'

He went into his tent, cleared a space and brought a stool. He would dictate the letter to

Eble whose hand was clear and fluent and he would allow him to choose the men to accompany him on the long journey to London to deliver it to their new king. Since his conversation with Alicia he had come to rely on his squire more and more and he had found him capable and efficient, and not the dreamer that he had always presumed him to be.

★ ★ ★

Eble ducked under the flap of the Earl of Lincoln's tent and watched as parchment and quills were brought in and laid on the table. Eble waited until they were alone again before quietly asking 'Does this mean the king is dead?' Henry nodded and Eble silently made the sign of the cross with a bowed head and closed eyes.

'I need you to scribe a letter and take it with all haste to Lord . . . to King Edward,' Henry corrected himself.

Eble took the quill in his hand and dipped it into the pot of ink, remaining patient as the earl paced the small tent, phrasing and re-phrasing what needed to be said. At length it was written, dried, sealed and packed away. Eble suggested the names of men he knew would ride with him, without complaint, and before the afternoon was through they had set off to make the most of what was left of the daylight hours.

Four days later, after riding hard, he was ushered into the presence of the king. From his knees he proffered the letter. 'Sire, I bring bad news.'

'Arise. Arise. I do not know you, do I? Are you one of Lincoln's household?'

'Yes, sire.'

'What is your name?'

'Eble le Strange, sire,' he replied, wishing that the king would open and read the letter that he held in his hands rather than studying him with interested and intense eyes.

'Then you have ridden from Scotland. How goes the war?'

'Sire,' said Eble, indicating the letter. 'Forgive me, but I think you should read it.'

The king opened the parchment and scanned it, then took it to the light of the window and read it again, his lips moving slightly as he whispered the words out loud. For a long time he did not move and then he turned back to Eble who was standing awkwardly, unsure what to do or how to behave.

'I am not sorry that he is dead,' said the king. 'I never really liked him and he did not like me. Bring wine and some refreshment for this messenger,' he told a servant then hesitated as he turned back to Eble. 'What should I do?' he asked, tapping the rolled parchment against the palm of his hand. 'I wish my brother Piers were here to guide me.'

'Sire, I believe that the Earl of Lincoln expects you to ride north to make arrangements for your father's body,' said Eble.

'Then that is what I shall do. Here, you must be rewarded for your good conduct,' said the king as he put down the letter to delve into the purse at his belt and bring forth a gold coin which he pressed with thanks into Eble's palm. 'Can I trust you, Eble le Strange?' he asked, still holding his hand. 'The Earl of Lincoln must hold you in high regard to send you on such a mission. Can I trust you to carry a letter for me?'

'Of course, sire,' said Eble, knowing that he could not refuse, but wary of the task that was to be set.

'I want you to take ship and go across the sea to Ponthieu. You must go to Piers Gaveston and bring him to me in Scotland. I will not be parted from him for another hour more than is necessary.'

*   *   *

Henry worried at his beard as he watched the young king present Piers Gaveston with the earldom of Cornwall. It was just over two weeks since Edward had arrived in Scotland and been proclaimed King Edward II at Carlisle Castle. The speed with which he had recalled Gaveston from France had amazed Henry and, although he had been reluctant to append his seal to the charter of enfeoffment that endowed Gaveston with lands and title, he was reluctant to fall out with the new king so early in his reign. But the closeness of Gaveston to the king worried him. He had seen how Edward had openly wept and embraced his friend in great joy when he had arrived in the north after his swift journey to their reunion. He did not entirely trust Gaveston and certainly did not like him. The supercilious smile that now adorned his face as he glanced in contempt at the gathered earls told him all he needed to know. Edward had already arranged a marriage between his niece, Margaret de Clare, and his friend and he currently seemed more concerned with the elevation of the man he called his brother than with the burial of his father.

Edward had left instructions that his body was to be boiled down to its bones and that his son was to carry those bones at the head of a great army and not to bury them until both Scotland and the Holy Land were conquered. The young king had snorted in derision when he had read his father's words and told Henry that the body was to be embalmed and taken south for burial at Westminster. Henry had asked what was to be done about Scotland, but young Edward had shaken his head uninterestedly and said that this was no time for fighting. He had then gone to celebrate his friend's return. Henry sighed. He would be glad when this day was over and he could take his leave to accompany the king's body on its journey south.

11

John de Warenne shifted anxiously in the saddle. All tournaments were fierce but this one was taking on all the features of a battle — one which they could not hope to win. In the official challenge that had been sent out by letter to all the earls and barons, Piers Gaveston had announced that he would hold the field with sixty knights against all comers. But a brief foray around the pavilions had revealed that his knights numbered nearer two hundred and there was little chance of victory for the opposing baronial team. John and the other earls had watched challenger after challenger knocked to the ground and the faces around him had become glummer with each resounding cheer from the Gascon camp.

John did not want to be here in the ward at Wallingford Castle, supposedly celebrating the marriage of Piers Gaveston to the king's niece Margaret de Clare. He did not want to joust against the Gascon and his knights, but the king had bid the earls attend and he had been left with little choice. The only thing that would have improved his mood was if his own team could have been victorious, but it was looking less likely with every run and now he was forced to face Gaveston himself in the lists.

The tall broad Gascon, dressed in green and seated on an equally tall and broad grey horse was intimidating and John felt a flutter of panic in his guts. Humphrey de Bohun, the Earl of Hereford, had only recently been helped, limping, from the field after Gaveston had knocked him squarely from his saddle and now it was his turn. He felt a trickle of sweat run down his temple and although it was December, and the day was cold, his hands felt slick within his gauntlets. If he had had the courage he would have turned and run, but instead he stayed motionless in the saddle to face the king's friend. He prayed that the man would show some mercy and not kill him.

'We're relying on you,' the Earl of Lincoln had told him, just before he crammed his helm onto his head and swung up onto his destrier. 'They are all too young for me now, so it's up to you show this damned upstart that he cannot best a true Englishman. Remember everything I have taught you.'

But would that be enough, he wondered. The golden spread eagles on the Gascon's banner seemed to mock him as they fluttered

117

against the greying sky and a shiver ran through him as he saw the herald drop his flag and his opponent heeled his horse and began the charge.

Mentally crossing himself, John weighed the lance in his hand, pressed it firmly against his side, then shouted 'Ha!' to encourage his horse on. The animal moved fluidly beneath him. All he had to do was keep his nerve, aim for the centre of Gaveston's shield and not strike until he was sure that he could knock the man from his saddle.

The wind whistled through his helm. He swallowed and tried to concentrate, telling himself that he could do it, that he wouldn't let the others down. He focused on the eagles on the shield coming towards him, but before he could make his move he had a sensation of everything around him becoming dark and muffled. Momentarily he was flying and then he was gasping and struggling for breath. Someone pulled off his helm and he saw the flash of a horse's hooves perilously close to his face. For some reason his lungs didn't seem able to draw in air and for a moment he thought he was dying. Then he began to pant as if he had been running for a long, long time and the numbness was replaced by a jarring pain through his chest from back to front. As he regained his senses he saw

Gaveston saluting the crowd with his shattered lance and as his squires helped him to his feet the pounding of blood in his ears faded to the sound of laughter as he staggered from the lists, spitting blood and cursing the Gascon with every filthy word he knew in both French and English.

★　★　★

Lady de Vescy paused mid-stitch as the unexpected sound of laughter drifted up from the courtyard below. There was no mistaking the king's deep voice, even though his laughter was a rare thing. She put her tapestry aside and went to the window. Edward was with Piers Gaveston and she watched as the king put his arm around his friend's shoulders as they continued to share some joke between them. In all the years she had known Edward she had rarely seen him laugh without restraint as he was doing now. He had always been a shadow of a boy, afraid of his father, constantly striving to please him yet always seeming to disappoint. His father had wanted him to be a copy of himself — fierce, war-like, independent. But the boy had always been unsure of himself. He had craved affection, though he had never received it, and Lady de Vescy could understand why Piers Gaveston held such an attraction for him.

She recalled the first time Gaveston had come to court with his father. He and Edward must have been about fifteen years old then and the friendship between the boys had been instantaneous. As soon as Edward had set eyes on Piers he seemed to change, as if something that had been asleep within him for a very long time had been wakened. And Piers had never been obsequious in the way that other members of Edward's household had been. From the very beginning he had treated Edward as his equal. It had made him enemies amongst those who thought he should show more respect, but Edward had loved him for it. The friendship had grown stronger and stronger and the boys had been inseparable until Piers was sent away.

Lady de Vescy had not been surprised when Edward's first act as king had been to send for his friend. There was a bond between them, not just the oath to become blood brothers, but a deeper connection. It was as if they were joined by some invisible thread that held them together no matter how far the distance between them, and when they were in one another's company it was strengthened and renewed.

'Here comes Monsieur le Burst Belly!' said

Piers and Lady de Vescy was annoyed at his insolence as she saw him point towards Henry de Lacy who was dismounting from his horse. She didn't hear Edward's reply, but there was a fresh burst of laughter as they moved away. She watched as Henry greeted the king and glanced with irritation at Piers who showed no sign of leaving the king's side.

She moved away from the window and sat down again, wondering what had brought Henry and how long it would be before he was finished with his business. It was not as long as she expected before there was a ripple of noise in the doorway and a servant announced the Earl of Lincoln. He kissed her cheek in a distracted manner and, ignoring the cup of wine she offered, he went to stand near to the fire.

'Problems?' she asked as she watched him rub the side of his face with his hand as if it ached.

'What do you make of Gaveston?' he asked her.

'He . . . ' She hesitated and tried to find a way to describe her complicated opinion of the young Gascon. 'He makes Edward laugh,' she said after a moment, 'and it is pleasing to see him happy. God alone knows the boy has not had much happiness in his life so far.' She glanced up at Henry and remembered the name that Piers had called him. 'His humour is not to everyone's taste,' she admitted. 'He has a vicious tongue at times but I don't think it comes with any real malice.'

'But do you not think that he has too much influence over the king?' asked Henry.

'I'm not sure. Edward promotes him, and he certainly listens to his opinion. They are very close.'

'Too close,' muttered Henry. 'I came to speak to the king about his marriage,' he said. 'The king of France is anxious that it should go ahead soon. If it does not there could be danger of another war — and we cannot afford that. But I've had the devil of a job persuading Edward to even discuss the matter.'

'Would you like me to speak to him?' she asked.

'Will he listen to you?'

'If I can catch him at the right moment, and in the right mood.' It was like trying to catch a cloud, she thought. Edward was elusive and moody and you were never sure how he would react. And speaking to him without Piers Gaveston would be even more difficult. But she agreed with Henry that the marriage needed to go ahead for the sake of the country. There was little money left in the coffers and to risk the treaty that had been made with the French would be foolish. But there was something about the way that Edward had put his arm around his friend that she found troubling. She said nothing to Henry, but she began to wonder just how deep the friendship between the king and his companion was, and how a wife would be received by either of them.

★   ★   ★

'The Earl of Lincoln has begged me to speak to you, sire,' said Lady de Vescy as Edward took her hand to lift her from her curtsey and lead her towards the bench by the hearth. The king lifted an enquiring eyebrow, but it was towards Piers Gaveston he looked and a smile spread across the Gascon's face.

'Sent a woman to do a man's work,' he remarked and Edward laughed.

'It is on a private matter,' she said.

'I have no secrets from my brother Piers,' replied Edward. 'You may speak freely in front of him.'

Lady de Vescy watched as Gaveston settled himself onto a stool. He oozed wealth and class and his clothes were not dissimilar to those of the king. He flicked at the tassels on his expensive boots as he watched her. Edward remained standing and folded his arms across his chest. Amusement hovered around his lips as if there was some joke between the men and it was at her expense. She felt unsettled and a little cross, as if they were making fun of her.

'The Earl of Lincoln has asked me to speak to you about your marriage to Isabella of France. He is keen that there should be no more delay.'

'Ah. The child bride,' replied Edward with a glance towards his friend.

'Well she is French — which must be an advantage,' said Piers.

'And do you recommend all things French?'

'You have not complained about the French I have taught you so far.'

'So far? Do you mean that you have more to teach?'

'You would be surprised at the length and depth of what I know,' replied Piers with a slow smile.

'My lord.' Lady de Vescy called for Edward's attention although the king continued to gaze at his friend as if they were the only two people in the room. 'Sire!'

'Yes, my lady,' said Edward at last. 'I hear you. The Earl of Lincoln has sent you to beg that I marry the child.'

'She is twelve years old.'

'Half my age. Does the earl expect me to bed her as well?' he asked. 'Or is this merely a political alliance?' He sounded bored and Lady de Vescy became impatient. She knew that Edward could be both difficult and stubborn, but in the past he had listened to her counsel and shown her some respect. But now he seemed to be enjoying trying to belittle her in front of his friend. The men were exchanging sly glances and flittering smiles and she clenched her hands together to contain her anger.

'I think that twelve years old may be too young for the marriage bed,' she replied. 'But the king of France is keen for the wedding to take place. Surely that is better than another war?'

'Oh we don't want another of those,' shuddered Edward. 'I do not like wars. What do you think, Perrot?' he asked, turning to his friend and using his pet name as if there was no one else present.

Gaveston shrugged, spreading his hands so that his sleeves hung stylishly from his wrists. His fingers flashed with jewelled rings.

'Will it make a difference?' he asked.

'To us? Of course not. She will be . . . she will be here, at court, that is all.'

'Then I shan't have to fight her for my place in your affections?' His voice trailed away and Lady de Vescy averted her eyes. Her suspicions had been confirmed but she had no wish to know the intimate details.

'May I tell the Earl of Lincoln that you are agreeable then?' she asked, her voice more strident than she had intended.

'If you must,' said Edward with a sigh and dismissed her with a wave of his hand, and when she glanced back from the doorway she saw that Piers was by the king's side, his hand moving comfortingly over his back as if he had been dealt some painful blow.

★ ★ ★

As the date of the king's marriage drew near, Thomas took to his bed and pleaded illness. I was unsure if it was genuine or brought on by the melancholy that often struck him when affairs did not play out in his favour. His self-importance had grown after the death of the old king. He was second in line to the throne, and was watchfully eyeing that throne for himself despite his outward show of support and affection for his cousin. When he refused to get up and insisted that his physicians attend him in his bedchamber I wondered if Edward's decision to marry had caused his unease. I suspected that he had been hoping the king would refuse to comply and that the betrothal would be broken. It would have meant war with France and I think my husband had a vision of himself riding to the rescue of England whilst the king and his favourite cowered like virgins before the dragon. He thought that he would prove to be victorious and that the earls would turn naturally to him as their leader and that the king would be put quietly away somewhere where he could do no harm. But it was a dream on Thomas's part and nothing more. I had seen him ride in tournaments and in the tiltyard at Pontefract and I knew that if he were to be victorious it would be dependant, not on his own skills, but on the skills of those who rode with him.

I did not visit him in his chamber and he did not send for me. It was peaceful whilst he was busy with his sulking and I could ignore the comings and goings of his physicians and attendants by keeping to my own apartment. But as the date for the marriage drew nearer I became anxious — not on my husband's behalf, but because I had been looking forward to attending and I was unsure if Thomas would allow me to accompany my father without him.

When a messenger arrived from the king, his cloak covered in a powdering of snow, I hoped that whatever the letter said would persuade my husband from his bed, and I was on the verge of consulting with my maid, Edith, about what garments I would need to pack when I heard Thomas's angry voice reverberating around the stairwell.

Edith and I held one another's gaze in a moment of anxiety before the door was thrust open and my husband strode in waving a parchment. His anger rendered him incapable of any coherent speech apart from obscenities and at first I could make no sense of what he was saying. I only hoped that his fury might cause him to fall dead at my feet so that I would no longer have to endure him.

'Gaveston!' he repeated. His face was flushed and his eyes were uncharacteristically bright, though whether it was from fever or anger I could not tell. 'Gaveston!' he repeated. 'Keeper of the Realm! It would not surprise me, my lady, to find that your father has put him up to this!'

I sat on the bench and watched as he stormed and bellowed, flinching as he flung a cup into the hearth where it clanged against the fire dogs before beginning to glow in the flames. In his fits of anger Thomas always laid the blame on my father and that in turn meant that I was forced to bear the brunt of his rage, and sometimes his fists as well if he thought that any word I uttered, or any expression that crossed my face, was in defiance of him.

I cowered as he approached me and grasped my braid in his hand, pulling up my bowed head and forcing me to look at him.

'I will never let him forget this! This apology for a king and the jumped-up Gascon knave! I will not be insulted in such a fashion!'

'No, my lord,' I whispered, praying that he would leave me alone, wishing that I could go to France instead of having to remain here with him and his temper.

'I will never bow to the will of men like them!' he bellowed in my ear as if it were entirely my fault. I lowered my eyes and he pushed me away from him. I slid from the bench onto the floor as he stamped out and slammed the door behind him, causing a cold wind to rustle the floor rushes and sputter the flames of the fire with black smoke.

'My lady!' Edith put a hand under my arm to help me up. 'Are you all right?'

'Am I ever all right when my husband is at home?' I asked her, reaching up to straighten my hair and pin my braid around my head. 'He is an idiot,' I said. 'Did he ever think that the king would appoint him keeper when he claims he cannot even rise from his sickbed?

It is his own fault if his petty spite has turned on him like a mad dog and bitten him.'

★   ★   ★

I was filled with a sense of foreboding as the scent of the dried flowers, scattered on the ground outside the abbey, lent a promise of springtime to that cold, February day. My mother's health worried me. She was so thin that I could count her bones and yet her belly was swollen with the monster she was convinced grew within her. Fear gnawed at me that she would not see the spring, and every moment I spent in her company was precious.

She had insisted on coming with me to the coronation. She leaned on me and I had to find a place where she could sit down. She would not be able to see everything that would occur, but the celebration would go on some while and I was anxious that she would become too tired if she had to stand.

My husband and my father were both taking part and so had been gone since early morning. They had both been tight-lipped and, for once, in agreement. I knew that they were angered by the favour that the king bestowed on Piers Gaveston. He had been given an earldom although he was not royal by birth, was not even English. It was inappropriate for him to take such an exalted role. But the king was adamant and would not be denied his friend.

I watched as the procession came slowly forwards: William Marshal carrying the gilt spurs, the Earl of Hereford with the royal sceptre, Henry of Lancaster with the royal rod, then my father and husband with the Earl of Warwick carrying the three swords of state. Then came the royal robes, carried on a board covered in chequered cloth, and Walter Reynolds with the paten and John Langton with the chalice of St Edward the Confessor. Then came Gaveston. His splendour made even my robes look shabby and although the other earls wore cloth of gold in the presence of the king, Gaveston wore royal purple, of silk, and encrusted with jewels. Preceding the king and queen he carried the royal crown as if he were, after them, the most important in the kingdom. It was little wonder that Thomas was so angry and for once I had some sympathy with his rage.

King Edward came into the abbey barefoot. Beside him walked Queen Isabella. They made offerings of gold at the altar. Edward was anointed and Bishop Woodlock placed the crown upon his head. Then he was escorted to his gilded and painted throne, beneath which was placed the rough-hewn rock of the Scottish kings. I watched as the line of earls knelt before him and swore homage and fealty. But as the king and queen left the abbey, having received the sacrament, Piers Gaveston, rather than my husband Thomas, carried the sword Curtana before them and there were shouts of discontent from amongst the assembled congregation.

When, long after darkness had fallen, the wedding banquet was eventually laid before us, it was cold and quite inedible. I lifted a morsel of the meat to my nose and sniffed. It did not smell good and when I examined it further between my fingers I found that the hardened and burnt outer portion hid a pink and barely cooked interior. Around me others were doing the same, some taking the meat discreetly from their mouths and dropping it for the dogs, or rats, below. I think that by the time the tables were cleared there was as much remaining on the platters as had been borne in. People whispered that it had been done purposely by the cooks to shame Piers Gaveston, who had been responsible for the arrangements.

At the top table I saw the little queen yawn with exhaustion. The king was busy laughing and drinking with his friend and had left her quite alone. As I rose from my place to see what could be done I saw Lady de Vescy approach her and take her hand. The queen was taken away to her bed and the king continued to laugh and drink, and did not even notice that she had gone. My father came to join us and Thomas spat that he was minded to make war on his cousin if he did not banish Gaveston for good. And for once my father did not disagree with him.

12

My lady mother died at Pontefract that spring, in a chamber that overlooked the courtyard where my brother John had plunged to his death. I sat beside her and held her frail and cold hand as she slipped from this world and it gave me some comfort to know that she would soon be with my brothers and my sister. I imagined them coming forward to take her hands and lead her towards heaven. She had made her confession to the priest and been shriven and I believed that she would not have to dwell in purgatory.

My husband had allowed me to go to her when the messenger arrived from my father saying that she was not expected to live much longer, and for once I was grateful for his swift dismissal of me as he had waved a hand to say that I could leave before turning his attention back to the whore who was perched upon his knee. She had smirked at me, then put out her tongue as I watched him plunge his hand beneath her skirts and lower his lips to her bared breast. I had turned from the spectacle, thinking that she was welcome to him and that if it kept him from my bed then I did not care where he took his sport.

After my mother had taken her last shallow breath and lay still my father knelt beside her body for a long time. He did not speak, or weep, or make any sound at all until, at last, a slight sigh escaped his lips and he leaned to kiss her motionless face.

'I loved you Margaret,' he whispered as if he needed to convince her that it was so. 'I loved her,' he told me as he rose stiffly to his feet, pushing himself up with a hand on the bedframe, and his face was so filled with anguish that I opened my arms to him and he held me tightly as he used to do when I was child. 'But she would not love me anymore,' he added as a sob wrenched his body. 'And I tried, Alicia. God knows that I tried. Do not judge me too harshly.'

I followed him down the steps to the hall. A servant brought wine but then withdrew. We were left alone with our grief before the crackling, smoky hearth. I found it hard to accept that what I had seen was real — that it was not one of the nightmares that plagued my sleep. In the bailey everyone was still going about their business. The blacksmith was fitting a steaming hot shoe to the hoof of a grey horse. Some barrels of wine were being unloaded from a wain. A woman was driving a flock of geese to the pasture. I could not comprehend that my mother was no longer part of this world, that I would never see her smile or hear her laugh again, never sit and listen to her stories as we embroidered a tapestry side by side on the window seat.

I saw tears dropping into my cup like sudden raindrops into a puddle and did not even know that it was me who wept until I heard my sobs break the silence. The cup was taken from my hands and I was in my father's arms again. He was warm and soft and he kissed my head, but I could feel his body racked with weeping too as we held and comforted one another.

★ ★ ★

My mother was scarce cold in her tomb before men began to ingratiate themselves with my father. They murmured words of sympathy on our loss before introducing their daughters — soft-skinned girls whose curving figures showed all the promise of healthy children. Some cast me contemptuous looks as if my barrenness offended them, whilst others seemed to smile in certainty that boys would spring from their wombs — boys who would take precedence over me. It must have troubled my husband too. He expressed his sympathy, then tried to dissuade my father from considering another wife. But I knew that my father yearned for a living son and I knew that he would not relinquish his last chance.

The news that my father was to marry Joan de Martin made my husband very angry. 'It is you who should provide an heir for your father's lands,' he shouted at me after reading the letter. And that night he came to my chamber and sent away my women. He did not even wait for me to undress but pushed me down on the bed, pulled up my skirts and rammed himself into my body again and again as I pleaded with him to stop. Whilst he thought my father would have no more children he had been biding his time until my father died so that he could claim his lands and then either put me away in a nunnery or arrange for me to meet with some accident. 'Your family seem very prone to misfortune,' he would tell me with an edge of threat in his voice whenever I said or did something that displeased him. Now that my father was to marry again he worried that he might lose what he considered was rightfully his — and unable to punish my father he punished me instead. But from such brutal encounters no child ever grew and it made him angrier still.

Henry de Lacy caught the look of distaste on the face of his new wife as pulled his tunic over his head. Although Joan relished her status as the Countess of Lincoln, and all the privileges that came with it, she was not the willing wife he had hoped for, or the one which her father had promised him she would be.

Was he so unattractive, Henry wondered as she averted her face. It was true that over the years his body had grown a little rounder, but he was still fit, could still ride a horse and was capable of using his lance to good effect in the joust, and in battle too if it should be necessary. And he knew how to please a woman. Had Bella not told him so?

Joan had composed herself now and lay on her back, head on the bolster with the sheets pulled demurely to her chin. He knew that she would make no protest if he pulled the covers from her and fondled her body, but neither would she return the attention by holding or kissing him. She would lie there as a yielding but passive partner with her eyes tightly closed and Henry suspected that she prayed under her breath for him to be finished. No wonder she did not quicken with child when she refused to abandon herself to the joy of the act. And if her coldness made him yearn for Bella's warm flesh then whose fault was that but her own?

It had all gone so wrong, he thought. It was never meant to turn out like this. Alicia had not given him a grandson and the girl who lay here in his bed, with a look of resignation on her face, showed no sign of bearing him another son. Margaret had died without them ever repairing the hurt between them and he had made Bella so angry that she would not remain in the same room with him.

'I will sleep in my own chamber tonight,' he said and saw the relief on his wife's face. I was once young like you, he wanted to shout at her, I was young with muscles like iron and I was never bested in a joust. My first wife used to moan with pleasure when I took her. She gave me two sons. Was it my fault that God took them away from me?

13

The laboured breathing of my father clouded the frosted air in his chamber. Despite the logs on the fire and the rugs on the bed the room was filled with cold and despair. As the soft chanting of the chaplains drifted in through the door, gusted upwards by some icy draught from below, I prayed that my father might recover his wits, but reason told me that he was dying.

On the other side of the bed Joan de Martin shifted restlessly. My father had been unfailingly kind to her, but I knew that she did not love him, and she had not even provided the house of de Lacy with another son. Her belly was as flat as the day they were wed. She looked bored. Her gaze roved the heavy beams of the ceiling as if seeking some inspiration, or a promise that it would soon be over and she would be free to leave. Aware of my reproachfulness she lowered her eyes to the figure on the bed.

My father did not look like my father. One side of his face drooped, beyond his control, the eyelid half shut and a dribble of saliva ran from his open mouth. I wiped it gently with a cloth. He had been like this for two days now and was sinking deeper and deeper into some world known only to himself, muttering and sometimes crying out as if in pain with a sound that cut to my own soul and made me weep for his suffering. He did not deserve this.

Father Giles came quietly into the chamber and closed the errant door behind him, shutting out the sound of the psalms from below. He had the holy oil in his hands and I moved aside so that he could perform the last rites for my father — his last service to him in this world, apart from the prayers he would say for his soul after he was dead. He laid a hand on my head in blessing and said some words that sounded reassuring but were not. I did not want my father to go to the arms of his maker, to a better place, to eternal glory. I was very afraid of what would happen if he were not here to protect me.

I blamed the king. He had made my father so angry. When he had told him that he was going to move the exchequer to York my father had told him he would resign as keeper of the realm. I knew that he was in despair. He feared for the future. In the end the king had relented and my father was reconciled with him. But he knew that before long there would be some other trouble, some new scheme thought up by Piers Gaveston to which the king would agree without question.

My father had invited Thomas and me to the house at Kingston in Dorset where he had kept Christmas with his new wife. The men had talked of nothing but the ways in which they could control the king and stop him being the puppet of Gaveston. My father had grown red faced and angry as they had talked and he had complained endlessly about the way the king and his favourite treated him. I had begged Joan to take him aside and distract him to keep him calm, but she had shrugged and said it was not her place to tell her husband what he should do. I wondered if she encouraged his anger. Perhaps she had always hoped that it would end like this and that she would be widowed and rich — a pleasing prospect for a younger man.

As the priest finished his ministrations, I heard footsteps and voices beyond the door and I rose from my knees to see what the trouble was. I recognised Lady de Vescy at once and told Eble le Strange that she might be admitted. I knew that she had been my father's mistress and I would not prevent her from seeing him one last time. She came in with tears on her cheeks.

'How is he?' she whispered.

I shook my head, wordlessly, as she went to the bedside. Joan stared at her.

'Let us go into the garden for a few minutes and breathe some fresh air,' I said. 'We will give Lady de Vescy a moment alone to say goodbye.'

★ ★ ★

At his death my father was the regent of all England. Whilst the king was fighting in Scotland he alone had ruled the country with his usual benevolence and care. But my father was barely placed in his tomb at St Paul's before my husband began to act as if he were indeed the king. He refused to go into Scotland to pay homage to Edward for his lands and insisted that the king come south to him at Haggerston Castle. He seemed determined to destroy Edward and set about hurting him where he was most vulnerable — in his affection for Piers Gaveston.

My husband began to gather around himself a loyal circle of those who would bow to his will and defy the king. They came on horseback, with many men-at-arms and servants and filled the castle at Pontefract with talk, and dogs that snapped and snarled at one another in a reflection of the jostling and posturing amongst their masters. They sat around hearths and trestles with cups in their hands and rebellion on their minds as they busied dozens of scribes to make copies of the ordinances which they planned to present to the king to curb his power, so that he would have no more control over his crown than the lords of misrule on the twelfth night. Thomas told me nothing but I was used to being quiet and listening. It was a skill I had learned from my father and he had taught me well. As I sat and sewed or oversaw the feeding of so many visitors I learned more and more about my husband's ambition and I understood that he intended to rid himself of the Gascon for good. The king he thought he could manipulate, but never Gaveston; he was cleverer than my husband and a better jouster — and I saw that Thomas hated him.

★ ★ ★

Isabella de Vescy put down the harp and went to stand beside the king; the music had not soothed him as it would have done his father. She rested a hand on Edward's head as he sat and buried his face in his palms and sobbed and cursed and swore. He was the nearest thing that she had ever had to a child of her own and she yearned to bring him some comfort.

'They seek to rob me of my power and they have fabricated these things from spite,' he said, showing her the list of demands that the Lords Ordainers had presented to him. 'They tell lies about Piers, and accuse him of leading me astray and giving me bad counsel. You don't believe that, do you?' he asked, looking up at her with glistening eyes. She didn't reply. 'They demand that he is cast out, not only from England, but from all my kingdoms — forever and without return. I have begged them,' he told her. 'I have said that I will agree to their demands, no matter how much it is to my disadvantage, if only they will stop persecuting Piers. What will I do without him?'

'I know that you love Piers,' she said, 'but I do not think you can fight the will of the earls. They are determined.'

'John de Warenne supports me,' argued the king.

Perhaps he only seeks your favour because he hopes you can influence the matter of his divorce, thought Lady de Vescy. Besides, she knew how much John de Warenne hated Thomas of Lancaster and she believed that he would have made a pact with the devil himself in an effort to oppose to him.

'Perhaps,' she said gently, 'it is time for you to find a place in your affections for the queen. I believe that she loves you, and if Piers were not here you might grow closer to her.'

'Even you think he should be sent away!'

'No,' she soothed as she saw his temper rise. 'But there are some things that even a king cannot prevail against. Remember that the subjects of King Canute believed that he could turn back the tide, but he could not — and I think you may not be able to turn back the tide of these demands. If you wish to retain your crown you may have to accept that you must be parted from Piers. At least he will be safe if he is sent abroad,' she warned him. 'For I do not think he will be safe if he remains here.' Edward stared up at her without speaking. 'If you truly love him you may have to let him go,' she advised.

Part Two — 1317 to 1322

14

John de Warenne walked around his horse, checking the girth and the stirrups and the bridle for himself. He knew that he could never be too careful. A loosened strap or a faulty buckle could cause a serious accident — even death. Having assured himself that his horse was properly prepared he nodded to the squire and put a foot to the stirrup before swinging up onto the destrier. With the advantage of greater height, he glanced towards the pennants that were flying over the tents on the other side of the lists and wondered if Eble had come. He would like to hear his friend's counsel on whether or not he should allow himself to become embroiled in the plot to find and arrest Piers Gaveston.

Although the king had forbidden this tournament, Thomas of Lancaster and most of the other earls had gathered in defiance of him and John was well aware that it was not sport, but plots that were the reason. He felt uneasy about being here at all. He wanted no part in this growing rebellion against Edward, but Archbishop Winchelsey had persuaded him that it might be to his advantage to come.

John had gone to see the archbishop, yet again, to argue his case for an annulment of his marriage so that he could marry his mistress, Maud de Nerford, and although the man had made no promises he had made it clear that if John were to assist in the matter of Piers Gaveston then he might be more willing to help, using the argument that John was under twenty-one years old when he married and so could not have properly consented to it. The archbishop had said that Gaveston was an evil man who had bound the king to him by sorcery, an assertion that had almost caused John to laugh out loud until he saw that the priest was in earnest. In the end he had agreed to attend the tournament, but he still had doubts — doubts about whether he should join the witch-hunt against Piers, and doubts about his own safety. He had had a nightmare again the previous night. It had unsettled him and the old nerves beset him as he urged his horse towards the lists, and the animal responded to his fears with a skittish dance across the muddied grass.

John understood why Piers Gaveston had returned to England, even though his banishment was supposed to have been final.

His young wife Margaret had borne him a daughter at York and he understood Piers' need to see the child. He had felt the same when his own son had been born. The thrill of holding a baby that had sprung from his own body was something that he could not find the words to explain. It had made him want to laugh and cry at the same time and as he had kissed the furrowed little brow he had sworn that he would find a way to make the child his legitimate heir.

Whether Gaveston had intended to stay or whether he had thought to see his wife and daughter and then slip back to a ship somewhere along the coast, John did not know. But whatever his intention, Edward had taken the decision to revoke his exile and had made a declaration that he had returned by the king's order and that the king held him good and loyal. It had sent the ordainers into a frenzy, especially when Edward had met with supporters in York and told them that he revoked everything he had agreed to. The earls had met in London and although they had been reluctant to wage war against the king, they had agreed to arrest and try Piers Gaveston for treason.

John had not been there. He had always declined to be involved with Lancaster's ordinances and had spent the previous summer in Scotland with the king. He had found Piers to be charming and witty. He was good company and his mimicry of Thomas of Lancaster was far more entertaining than anything the king's minstrels had performed. It was Piers' acerbic tongue, the fact that he was a foreigner and that he wore his clothes so well that made the other earls so angry, thought John. He did not blame the king for listening to his friend's advice rather than that of Lancaster, everyone knew that everything Lancaster suggested was designed to curb the king's power and increase his own.

He ought to have stayed away, thought John as he circled the impatient horse and squinted through his visor to see who his opponent in the lists might be. He should have gone home to Conisbrough and Maud and watched to see what would happen. If it hadn't been for the half-promise of the annulment he would have done. It was only because he was determined to make Maud his wife that he was here at all, ready to joust against Lancaster's best knights, and then be persuaded to take part in Gaveston's arrest.

★ ★ ★

John shaded his eyes against the May sunshine as he looked across the rippling water of the North Sea to where boats belonging to the Earl of Pembroke patrolled the shoreline. The castle at Scarborough had not been stocked for a siege, had received no supplies for over a week, and earlier that day a messenger had been sent out under a flag of truce to say that Gaveston was willing to discuss terms for his surrender.

A movement at his side made John turn and Aymer de Valance, the Earl of Pembroke approached. His serious expression gave his dark face a more sombre countenance than usual and John wondered what had taken place within the high stone walls.

'He is asking to see you,' said Pembroke. 'Apparently my promise alone is not enough, though I have told him that he will not be harmed.' John nodded. The request to speak personally to him was not unexpected and he knew that his role in this affair was to persuade the man to give himself up.

Inside, Piers Gaveston was sitting on a chair on the dais. He showed no sign of the effects of the ten day siege as he beckoned John forward in his usual manner, as if he were a servant. John pursed his lips and frowned. Gaveston did himself no favours.

'My lord,' he said with a brief nod of his head.

'Pembroke,' said Gaveston, indicating the

153

earl with a sweep of his bejewelled hand, 'tells me that he will escort me to St Mary's Abbey in York, and that if the king and the Earl of Lancaster cannot come to terms by the first day of August I will be returned here.'

'That is correct, my lord.'

'And you will swear an oath to guarantee my safety?'

'You have my personal promise,' said John.

It seemed to satisfy Gaveston and he stood slowly, stretching his arms and legs as if he had just woken from a deep sleep.

'Perhaps you would be good enough to send in some food so that I may eat before we travel,' he said and John saw the Earl of Pembroke nod his assent to two of his men-at-arms.

'You will ensure he is kept safe?' he asked Pembroke as Gaveston strolled off to prepare himself for the journey. 'Now that I have done my part I want no more involvement. I am going back to Conisbrough.'

'You have my solemn oath,' said Pembroke.

★ ★ ★

As soon as he began to read the letter, less than a week later, John knew that he had been a fool. He should have stayed to protect Gaveston rather than leaving him in the care

154

of someone so stupid — or so corrupt. It would not have surprised him if a bribe had been an added attraction to that of the marriage bed which had resulted in Pembroke leaving his prisoner barely guarded at the rectory at Deddington from where the Earl of Warwick had snatched him.

John's hands trembled as he read the account of Gaveston's death — how he had been marched barefoot to Warwick Castle, held in the dungeon and given what amounted to no trial at all before being dragged out to Blacklow Hill, on Lancaster's lands, and brutally beheaded, his body abandoned by the roadside until it was taken to the Dominican friars at Oxford.

How was he to relate this to the king, he wondered with desperation, as the messenger stood by awaiting his reward for having ridden so quickly with the news. He fumbled in the purse that hung from his belt and gave the man two coins and dismissed him before reading the letter once more. Edward would have to be told, and though it was a task he would have pushed from him like a poisoned chalice, he knew that he could trust no other to be the bearer of such bad tidings. With dread and foreboding he walked to where the king and queen were lodging at the provost's house in the shadow of the great Minster at

Beverley where they had come to pray at the shrine of the saint.

'Your grace,' said John as he bowed to the king, the parchment still clutched in his clammy fingers.

'What is it?' asked Edward. 'Have the earls come up with yet more demands?' There was an edge of irritation in his voice and he raised an eyebrow as he waited for John to respond. 'Well?' he asked. 'What do they want now?'

The king held out his hand for the letter and John found that he was clutching it against him, reluctant to relinquish either the parchment or the news that it contained.

'It is bad news, your grace,' he said. 'Pray be seated.'

'Just tell me!'

'Sire, they have killed Piers Gaveston,' he said and watched as Edward appeared to shrink and crumble under the unexpected onslaught of his words

'Piers,' he replied, his voice tight with anguish. 'They have killed Piers?' He shook his head as if denying it could be true. 'Tell me it is not so.'

'I am sorry,' said John, although he knew the words were inadequate. Edward held out a trembling hand for the letter and sat down in the window embrasure to read it for himself. 'By God's soul!' he burst out, throwing the letter aside as a sudden rage enthralled him. 'What was he doing with the Earl of Warwick? This is what I always told him not to do! I knew that this would happen! I knew for certain that if the earl caught him, Piers would never escape from his hands! I will have Warwick's head for this!' vowed the king. 'And my cousin Lancaster will not go unpunished!' he raged before suddenly dropping his face into his palms and weeping as if he would never be consoled.

15

I was fearful as I approached the door of the privy chamber. I did not know why Thomas had summoned me. I prayed that I had done nothing to anger him. Since the death of my father he had taken to punishing me harshly.

Inside, I saw a parchment spread across the table. It was the plan for some building and Thomas waited, pretending to study it, before he spoke to me.

'Pickering,' he said briefly.

'My lord?'

'I have decided to have a new hall built for you there,' he told me.

'For me, my lord?'

'I am aware that you are unhappy here,' he said, 'and I think that it would be better if we lived apart.'

'Do you mean to seek a divorce, my lord?' I asked.

'Oh no,' he replied. 'I shan't divorce you, Alicia. I shall not break my agreement with your father or the vows of our marriage.' He smiled slyly. 'I will spare no expense,' he said, 'and Pickering is a pretty place.'

But remote, I thought, as I was forced to

express my gratitude. His decision demeaned me. I knew that I was being sent away to where I would have no part in the affairs of the de Lacy lands.

★ ★ ★

Without a word from me, my husband arranged for my belongings to be packed up for the journey. I was afraid that he would send one of his trusted men to watch me as a gaoler watches his prisoners. I wanted to ask who would accompany me, but I dared not. So the relief when I saw Eble le Strange at the door of my chamber was so great that I almost ran to him and clung around his neck. He came forward and knelt before me.

'I am to go with you to Pickering,' he told me. I reached down and touched his shoulder with my fingers.

'Please. Get up.'

Our eyes met and his were the colour of the sea on a sunny day and I saw the regard he had for me in the intensity of his look.

'For once my husband has made a good choice,' I told him. Thomas could never hurt me as he intended by sending Eble to oversee my household. For the first time in weeks I smiled, knowing that my banishment would not be without its compensations.

Eble jumped back as the basket at my feet let out a sound like the howling of some devilish spirit. A striped paw pushed through a gap in the wickerwork and clawed at the air, narrowly missing his blue woollen cloth of his hose and the softer flesh of his leg beneath.

'Hush, Tabby,' I soothed. 'You must stay in your basket. It's my pet cat,' I told Eble. 'He doesn't like to be shut up like this, but it would break my heart if I were to lose him on the journey. I know he must go on the baggage wagon, but will you promise me to take special care with him?'

I picked up the basket and held it out to him. He took it and held it at arm's length to avoid the animal's sharp claws

'I'll make sure he is safe,' he promised, and I knew he would. I had persuaded my father to trust Eble and I knew that I could trust him too. He was a good man.

★　★　★

When we arrived at the new hall at Pickering it smelt of damp plaster work. Even though the shutters were pushed wide open to allow in the air everything was so clammy from the continuous rain that the walls had not dried out, and the kindling and logs that were laid in the hearth were too damp to catch light.

'Your private chambers are above, my lady,' said Sir John de Dalton, the constable, as he hovered nearby, eager to please.

The wooden staircase felt pleasingly secure as I climbed it, one hand on the freshly painted rail. Above the hall was a chamber, more than ample for my needs. Another fireplace, built into the wall, was decorated with plasterwork leaves and flowers, and painted in the bright colours of a summer meadow. Fresh rushes from the banks of the river cushioned the boards of the wooden floor, though I thought they seemed still damp. A low door led to a garderobe and there was also a latrine with a wooden seat. It was all well done and I was grateful that my husband was sufficiently concerned with outward appearances that he had not stinted on the construction of my new home and that to outward eyes it seemed he was concerned for my welfare.

I turned back to where the constable was standing clasping and unclasping his hands as he awaited my verdict.

'It is all as I expected,' I reassured him. 'Tell the men to carry in the coffers and the bed. And try to find dry wood for these fires,' I said as I took off my wet cloak and sought a peg on which to hang it.

The men came up with the frame of the

bed and began to peg it together. Their voices echoed off the bare walls. It would seem more like a home, I thought, once the tapestries had been hung and cushions placed along the window seats. And, as I sought to decide which hangings should go where, I thought that the one I had helped my mother stitch, the one that had accompanied me to Kenilworth as a bride, should be put up first. It had been packed away for so long that I scarcely remembered what it looked like.

Two men wrestled the thickest mattress from the bed up the steps directed by a gaggle of women who complained at their ineptitude. Behind them appeared Eble with Tabby, asleep in his basket.

'Is there anything else I can do for you, my lady?' he asked.

'There is a hanging I would like brought in,' I said. 'It is wrapped in a green cloth. Will you find it for me?'

As I watched Eble help to unroll the picture of the squire with his brace of birds who loved the lady on her white horse, tears overwhelmed me as I recalled the happy days when my mother and I had sat in the embrasure at Pontefract, working the image with our needles and threads.

'My lady? Are you unwell?' asked Eble. I shook my head.

'I was reminded of my lady mother,' I said. 'She loved this hanging. I recall it needed a lot of persuasion before she agreed to let me have it, yet in all these years it has never been hung.'

I knelt down at the edge of the tapestry and ran a hand across the stitches, feeling the love with which they had been placed there. 'I think she sewed it nearly all herself. I was not diligent in my work,' I said, although I could see the places where the stitches were less neat and knew that those were the ones I had done. I wiped my eyes on the ends of my sleeves and stared once more at the young squire about whom I had invented such stories, in the days when I still believed that true love existed. And as I looked at his fair hair and blue eyes I saw a reflection of the squire who stood watching me anxiously.

'It could be you,' I said to Eble with a sudden smile. He walked around its edge to study it from a different angle.

'Then you must be the fine lady on the white horse,' he said. 'She is very beautiful.'

For a moment silence hung in the chamber as the servants paused in their work and watched us. Eble offered me his arm to help me up but I declined.

'You speak with a courtly tongue,' I told him. 'Do you still write poetry?'

'I do, my lady.'

'And have you any that you might share with us after supper?'

'I daresay I might remember one or two, if pressed.'

'Then my ladies and I will look forward to your words,' I told him as I got to my feet and smoothed my gown.

That evening we gathered in the upper chamber and we lit beeswax candles as the sun went down and settled onto the new cushions to listen as Eble sang for us. I watched the swell of his chest as he drew breath to begin. His voice was rich and deep and his singing confident. It was as if the song took him and made him its instrument. The soaring melody that filled the chamber was beautiful to my ears, yet it held such notes of sweet bitterness as to bring tears to my eyes.

'Bird on a briar, bird on a briar, I am in love. Blithe bird, take pity on me. I am so happy when I see that maid in the hall. She is white of limb, lovely and true. She is the fairest flower of all. If only I might have her she would save me from all my sorrows. I would be steadfast and true. Joy and bliss would be new.'

And as he sang his hands were held out to the invisible bird as he implored its pity, and his face was anguished with his hopeless passion for the lady. As the last sweet note faded on the evening air, a breeze wafted the sound of a late blackbird fluting his reply in through the open window. Eble le Strange's eyes lingered for a moment on mine. Then he looked away and the ladies clapped their hands and the magic was suddenly dispersed as the flames of the candles flickered and the chatter of voices chased the music away.

The next morning dawned fine and the sun shone so I took the opportunity to go out hunting in the forest. I had brought a hawk with me from Pontefract, a pretty little merlin with a bluish sheen to his wings, and after days of confinement the bird was eager to fly. Once out onto open moorland I released it from my wrist and it shot high into the air as if fired from a bow and after a moment began to shadow a skylark, which continued to sing despite the chase. The notes of the smaller bird haunted me and I began to regret its sure demise when it suddenly plunged to the ground and my merlin, taken by surprise circled and called forlornly at its loss.

'I am not sorry the little bird got away, my lady,' said Eble who was riding beside me with a whip to keep the dogs under control.

I held up my hand and the little merlin returned and I rewarded it with a titbit of meat from my pouch.

'I feel as if I have escaped myself,' I confided in him.

'You deserve better, my lady,' replied Eble with an unexpected vehemence. 'Your husband treats you badly to send you away to this remote place.'

'Are you sorry to have been sent here to oversee my household?' I asked him.

'No, my lady. I am glad to be away from Pontefract.'

I was pleased to hear him say so. I could not help but see how straight he sat in the saddle, how gentle his fingers were on the horse's reins and how shapely his legs that pressed against the horse's flanks. I could not put from my mind the story of Lady Mellette, or the image on the tapestry, and I could not dismiss from my thoughts the idea that this was what it felt like to fall in love.

16

Lady de Vescy welcomed Jeanne de Bar at the door of the queen's chambers. The last time she had seen Jeanne was when she had stood beside John de Warenne and made her wedding vows. Her head had scarcely reached his elbow then and she did not seem to have grown much since, although seven years had intervened. She was a slight girl and it was easy to believe, as Warenne claimed, that the marriage had never been consummated.

She took Jeanne's hands in hers. Even though it was May it was still unseasonably cold and the girl felt chilled after her long journey from Yorkshire.

'Come to the fire,' she said.

'Come and sit beside me,' said the queen patting the cushioned bench.

Jeanne curtseyed and then sat down beside Isabella. The two were much of an age and Lady de Vescy knew that the queen had been eager for Jeanne to arrive. It would do them both good to have a friend.

'Call for some wine and wafers, Lady de Vescy,' said the queen, 'and afterwards I will have the nurse bring little Edward in. You will love him,' she told Jeanne. 'He can walk unaided now and has begun to talk.'

Once the refreshments had been served and Jeanne was warmed, the young prince was sent for. Isabella took the little boy from his nurse and laughed as he tried to grab at her necklace.

'I will never have a child,' said Jeanne as she watched. 'My husband wants to divorce me,' she whispered as if shamed by the word. 'He says that our marriage is false and should be annulled. What did I do wrong?' she asked. 'He never came to my bed. I would not have refused him if he had. I wanted to be a good wife to him, but he never liked me.'

'Hush, hush,' soothed, Lady de Vescy as she put her arm around the girl's shoulders. 'The fault does not lie with you. You have done nothing wrong.'

It must have been hard for Jeanne to live at Conisbrough Castle whilst her husband flouted his mistress and their illegitimate son beneath her nose, she thought. It surprised her that John de Warenne had behaved so badly. Henry de Lacy had always spoken well of him, despite his hatred for the boy's grandfather. Perhaps it was in his blood, she thought, so many young men seemed to be behaving badly since Henry's death.

'You are better off here with us,' said the

queen, reaching out to take Jeanne's hand. 'The king will take care of you and make sure that you want for nothing.'

'I shall not consent to a divorce. I will not be treated so,' Jeanne told them fiercely. 'He is my husband and I am the Countess of Surrey!'

★   ★   ★

When John de Warenne walked into the great hall at Pontefract Castle he saw Thomas of Lancaster sprawled in the ornate chair that had once belonged to Henry de Lacy. The self-satisfied grin on his face was reminiscent of the expression with which he had habitually greeted him when they were both squires. He felt his stomach lurch as it had in the old days and was angry with himself for allowing Lancaster to intimidate him.

John sat down as the lawyers began to spread parchments on the tables and the clerks sharpened their nibs in preparation. Lancaster watched with the look of a man who seemed vaguely amused at the proceedings and John, who had come into the hall with feelings of hope, found his optimism crawling away like a whipped dog. Nevertheless he met Lancaster's eye and gave a brief nod of his head before turning to his lawyer

169

under the pretence of checking some detail. He could feel Lancaster watching him and the enmity of his gaze made the hairs on John's neck and arms rise like hackles.

Gradually a silence fell over the hall and John's lawyer stood to put the case to the council of nobles who were seated along the high table.

'My lords,' he began after a slight clearing of his throat, 'we are gathered here today to hear the petitions of Sir John de Warenne, Earl of Surrey and of Maud de Nerford in the matter of the legality of Sir John's marriage to Jeanne de Bar. My lords, Sir John pleads a case of consanguinity as he and Jeanne de Bar are second cousins. Sir John also pleads that he was forced into the marriage against his will, having been under the age of twenty-one years at the time. My lords, Maud de Nerford pleads that she was pre-contracted to marry Sir John de Warenne which makes any other marriage invalid.'

With a nod of his head the man returned to his bench and John watched as Jeanne's Italian lawyer, paid for by the king, slowly rose to his feet.

'My lords,' he began with a shrug of his shoulders. 'The lady, Maud de Nerford, claims a pre-contract, yet she was married to one Simon de Derby. How can this be so?' he asked and John clenched his fingers hard into his palms as he heard the ripple of assent. 'And Pope Clement . . . ' The lawyer paused. 'Pope Clement granted a dispensation for the marriage, so there are no grounds for it to be dissolved.'

John kept his eyes fixed firmly on his boots as the arguments of each side were made. He was paying Jeanne two hundred pounds a year whilst the case was heard and had promised seven hundred and forty marks' worth of lands once the marriage was dissolved. No one could fault his generosity to her, but still she would not be persuaded to agree.

At last, when all the points had been made, the council withdrew to Lancaster's privy chamber to discuss the outcome. As they got up, stretching their stiffened legs and talking amongst themselves before making their way out of the hall, John watched with growing frustration. He and Maud had prepared their petitions well and had paid for the best advice they could get, but during the course of the morning he had seen how all the men on the council had looked towards Lancaster for guidance and he had begun to suspect that his old enemy might prevent this divorce from pure spite.

He went down the steps into the courtyard

to get some fresh air whilst he waited for the verdict and found himself walking towards the stables. There were still a few familiar faces amongst the grooms who were brushing down the horses or fetching nets of hay and buckets of water. Some greeted him, with more civility than they had when he was a boy. He would not have been surprised to turn a corner and come face to face with Eble — and nothing would have given him greater pleasure. He suddenly longed for the strong arms of his friend to embrace him and give him some comfort. But a letter he had received from Eble had told him that he would not be at Pontefract as he had been sent north to Pickering with the countess. His loss was Eble's gain, thought John. The tone of the letter had left him in no doubt about his friend's delight and it seemed that Lancaster had no idea about Eble's feelings for Alicia.

A tug on his sleeve made him turn and his page boy told him that the council had come to a decision and were awaiting his presence. With foreboding in the place of his former hope, John found that his legs felt as heavy as lead as he climbed the steps to the hall. Inside, one glance at Lancaster's face told him all he needed to know.

'We find that there is no case for divorce,'

he told him without even getting up from his chair. 'We find that you are living sinfully with your mistress and that you are both in peril of your immortal souls. I suggest that you put aside your mistress and allow your wife to take her rightful place in your affections.'

John stared at him and could not find any words to reply. He felt the anger rage like fire through his veins as he stared at Lancaster — a man who kept many mistresses, who had a reputation for defiling any pretty girl who caught his eye, who had sent his wife away to a remote hunting lodge. How dared he criticise and lecture him? How dared he prevent his divorce so that he could not marry the woman he loved?

John took a breath to steady himself, but before he could say anything Lancaster had indicated that the proceedings were over and John found himself alone amongst the clerks as they gathered their papers and inks. This was not the end, he vowed. He would not accept this decision. Damn Lancaster! He would find a way to pay him back for this.

17

I picked up Tabby and held my cheek against his soft fur. It was warm from where he had been basking in the sun, but the day was growing overcast now and the storm clouds were gathering in more ways than one. My husband had sent word that he was coming to Pickering Castle to hunt in the forest and the sound of the horns beyond the walls told me Thomas and his friends were on their way and would expect a plentiful feast for their supper.

Tabby squirmed from my arms as he sensed danger and I watched as his ringed tail disappeared around the edge of the stone wall. I went to greet my husband, as a good wife should. The men swarmed into the bailey, laughing and shouting. My husband was smiling as he dismounted, but his expression turned to a scowl as his eyes lighted on me.

'See that my friends get good wine and food. Then I wish to speak with you privately,' he told me and walked away.

After my visitors were provided for I went to him. I hesitated in the doorway of the best bedchamber trying to assess his mood. His muddied boots and cloak were strewn across the floor and he turned to stare at me with contempt written starkly across his dark features. After sending the page away he crossed the chamber in two strides and for a moment I was unsure what had happened. My ears rang and everything seemed black. Then the stinging pain began to burn my cheek where he had slapped me.

'Whore!' he spat. I stared at him in disbelief as my palm cradled the agony and my tongue explored my teeth to check that none had been loosened. 'Oh, don't pretend that you are innocent! It is the talk of the whole of Yorkshire!'

'My lord,' I began. 'I do not know what I have done to displease you.'

He snorted in disbelief and I thought he was about to strike me again as his face closed in on mine.

'Did you think that I would allow you to cuckold me?' he demanded.

'I do not know what you mean.'

'You and Eble le Strange. You have taken him as your lover.'

'My lord, I have not!' I protested.

'You deny it?' he spat into my face.

'Of course I deny it. It is not true!' I told him, taking a step back from his furious, contorted face.

'Liar!'

'I speak the truth.'

'Do not deny it Alicia! Did you think that I would send you here without someone I could trust to tell me what you do?'

'You set someone to watch me?' I asked, wondering who in my household was a traitor and a spy. Although what they had told my husband was untrue. Eble le Strange was not my lover. Even though I often wished that he was, I had not yet broken the vows I had made before God and man to keep myself for my husband only. I had been a faithful wife, even though he had been a faithless husband to me.

'So what do you say now?' he asked with a smirk of satisfaction.

'It is not true,' I protested again. 'I have done nothing wrong!'

'Liar!' he said again. 'You had better pray hard to God for your forgiveness.'

I was about to tell him that his soul was more in need of prayer than my own, but I knew that nothing I could say would make any difference. Besides, I thought, let him believe that I had a lover. Let him believe that another man could please me as he could not, that I would willingly give myself to someone else whilst he could only take me by force.

'Get out,' he muttered.

'My lord,' I replied with a slight curtsey, whilst clutching at my skirts to stop myself flying at him and scratching his eyes out.

At supper the butter ran out and Thomas blamed the shortfall on me, telling everyone that I was a lazy and incompetent wife. I felt my cheeks burn in shame at his words though my maid, Edith, laid a hand on mine and whispered that he was drunk and did not know what he was saying.

The next morning I was in the dairy and had just poured some cream into a barrel to make more when a shadow filled the doorway. Tabby, who had followed me in the hope of a small treat, flattened his ears and hissed and Thomas kicked out at the cat, catching him with the toe of his boot and making him yowl in pain.

'Stop it!' I shouted, trying to pick up the frightened animal to see if he was hurt, but his silky fur slipped through my hands and he vanished out of the door.

'Give me that necklace!' said Thomas and I stared at him, not knowing what he meant. Then I touched the string of jewels that I always wore around my neck, the one that had belonged to my grandmother and which she had given me on my wedding day.

'No!' I said. 'It's mine.'

'Give it to me!' he repeated. 'I had a wager

and I lost, so I have a debt that must be repaid.'

'Then pay with your own money!' I told him.

'Do you want me to beat you in public for everyone to see what a disobedient wife you are?' he asked, grasping my arm and pushing me around so that my back was to him. I felt him unclasp the necklace with his cold hands and the familiar weight of it was lifted from my neck leaving me feeling part undressed and vulnerable. I turned and stared at it, glistening in his hand.

'It is mine,' I repeated.

'Not any more,' he smiled, slipping it inside the pouch on his belt and ducking down under the low lintel of the doorway.

I stood and stared after him, scarcely comprehending what he had just done.

'You bastard! You whoreson!' I muttered as I picked up the dasher and began to pound it in and out of the cream. 'It was mine! It was mine!' And I worked and worked at the liquid until it began to form into butter, wishing that I could pound a stick into my husband instead.

I glanced up as another shadow fell across the doorway and I hesitated, the dasher motionless in my hands, dripping whey into the barrel. Had he heard me and come back to punish me? But it was Eble who came into the dairy, his face solemn and something wet in his hands. I stared at the object not knowing what it was.

'I am sorry,' said Eble, his face twisted with grief. 'I tried to get him out . . . '

It was then that I saw his sleeves were drenched up to the armpits. I dropped the dasher and ran towards him, hoping that what he held in his hands was not what I feared. The saturated fur looked black in the gloomy light, but I knew that it was Tabby. I stared at the still and lifeless body then stretched out my hand and felt a remnant of warmth.

'Do something,' I pleaded.

'I have tried,' said Eble. 'I have tried everything that I know, but it is too late. I was going to bury him and hope that you never discovered the truth . . . but then I thought that you would want to know . . . to see him one last time.'

'No,' I said, desperately trying to stroke life back into the cat. 'It cannot be. Did my husband do this?' I asked. 'I hate him! I hate him and I want him to burn in hell! Is that wicked of me?'

Eble shook his head. 'No,' he said. 'He is an evil man. He . . . '

'What?' I asked, looking up at Eble and

seeing that the anguish I saw there was not just for what my husband had done to my pet. 'What else?'

'He has ordered me to return to Pontefract with him. He is to send another man to head your household.'

I was silent for a moment. Then I laid my hand on Eble's wet sleeve. 'My husband has accused me of taking you as my . . . lover,' I said. The word felt odd yet delicious on my tongue. We both stared down at the body of the cat between us. Despite their unpromising first meeting Tabby had become fond of Eble and would entwine himself around his legs and stare up at him with enquiring eyes. I'd seen Eble scratch the cat on the top of his head, between his ears, and under his white chin. I'd also seen him slip Tabby titbits from the table and I had felt unreasonably jealous when he abandoned my lap for Eble's — but whether that was because I yearned to curl up close to my squire myself I could not say.

'Will you bury him?' I asked. 'Will you say a prayer and show me his grave?'

'Leave him, Alicia,' said Eble quietly. 'Leave your husband. I will help you. Do you remember when you told me the story of how your grandmother was abducted from her manor at Canford by John Gifford? Go there and I will find a way to come for you. I will

180

take you somewhere safe, somewhere where he will never be able to hurt you ever again.' He glanced through the doorway as we heard voices. 'Go to Canford, Alicia, and wait for me there.'

★   ★   ★

I cannot pretend that I did not leave Pickering Castle without some regrets. It had been my home for three years. The new hall was warm and familiar and to leave it to ride south through the damp and drizzle of those cold March days, when winter still clung to the upper reaches of the moors, was a wrench. If I had been able to ride with Eble beside me I could have faced my uncertain future with equanimity, but since he had left for Pontefract I had heard no more of him and I knew that it might endanger him if I were to make enquiries. But that did not mean he was far from my thoughts. His ghost haunted Pickering. As I knelt in the chapel I imagined that I could hear his voice outside in the courtyard; in the evenings I expected to hear his step on the stairs as he came up to my chamber to sing for me. But all I had of him was a small parchment on which he had written a poem. It spoke of hope and love, of new beginnings and the dawning of new days in the sun. I had it folded and tucked inside my chemise, against my bare breast, knowing that he had held it in his hand. It gave me courage as I rode across the bridge that spanned the moat and out onto the road that led to the south. It helped me keep the promise I had made to myself not to look back, but to ride forward into my future, whatever that held.

The tapestry with the hunting scene had been carefully rolled and wrapped in waxed cloth to protect it before being loaded onto the wain. I faced a long journey. Dorset was as far south as I could go without leaving England altogether. The roads were wet and mired in mud which coated the legs of the horses and splashed up onto my cloak and gown, and the man that my husband had sent to replace Eble was morose. William Fischer was his name and he had not wanted to escort me south, saying that he was not sure my husband would approve. I had told him that I did not care what my husband thought and I'd seen from his expression that he was going to be stubborn. But, soon after, the Scots had sent a raiding party south and the sheep that had been herded outside the castle walls to graze were all butchered and taken, although on this occasion the shepherd was spared.

'It happens all the time,' I had told William when he came, with a heavy tread, up the steps to give me the news. 'Today it is sheep, tomorrow who knows? They see we have stocks and provisions and they are hungry. They will do whatever they can to feed themselves — and they can hardly be blamed. I will not stay to be robbed of everything I have. No matter what my husband might think I am leaving and going south to Canford. If it pleases you to accompany me I will welcome your protection. But if you refuse to go, then I will go alone.' He had glowered at me then, knowing he had no choice, and he was glowering now as the dark clouds rolled down from the north and drenched us with their icy rain.

We passed close by Pontefract, but I insisted that we ride swiftly past the high walls that had once protected me. It was not only because I did not want an audience with my husband that I avoided the castle, I knew that if I rode into the familiar bailey and climbed the steps to the women's solar I would feel the presence of my mother and father and I would never want to leave. If William Fischer thought it odd, he did not argue when I said that the journey was a long one and we must cover as much ground as possible each day. Anyway, it was no secret that my husband and I hated one another.

I was exhausted by the time we arrived at Canford Manor. I could barely make sense of the world as I was helped down from the horse and went inside. William had sent men ahead and fires were burning and there were fresh rushes on the floors, but winter still clung to the thick, cold walls and there was a smell of dampness mingled with the wood smoke. As I sat by the hearth and tried to rub some feeling back into my numbed fingers, I looked around at the bare stone and wished that I knew where Eble was, so that I might send word to him that I had arrived.

18

John de Warenne did not know and did not care who his opponent was. All he could see through the slit in his helm was that he wore Lancaster's colours and that was enough to make him determined to knock the man from his horse. His anger gave him confidence, that and the fear that if he, himself, were killed he would spend eternity in hell, denied any entry into heaven by the pronouncement of the Bishop of Chichester that he was excommunicate 'for adultery and openly keeping a mistress'.

He centred himself in his saddle, ensured that his feet were firmly in the stirrups and then took the lance in his hand. The end was sharpened. Lancaster had decreed that this tournament should be fought à outrance and John was in the mood to kill. He circled the horse around to keep it moving until his opponent signalled that he was ready. John, too, raised his lance and the herald dropped his flag.

'Ha!' shouted John as his spurs pricked the horse's flanks and it sprang to a full gallop. He clenched his teeth and set his eyes on his opponent's shield, intending to strike it so full on and hard that the man would not be able to stay in his saddle. But all he saw was a flash of sparks as his opponent's shield deflected the blow.

'God's soul,' he muttered, as he pulled hard on the reins to stop his horse. He had to perform better than that.

Breathlessly he turned the animal and looked back. Lancaster's man was still in his saddle despite the blow and preparing himself for a second run. John threw his damaged lance to the ground and held out his mail clad hand for a new one. It glinted reassuringly in the sun. If he didn't unhorse the man this time he meant to kill him. That would show Thomas of Lancaster that he could not make a fool of him, either in the courtroom or in the lists.

'Ha!' The horse leapt forward under him. The wind whistled through his visor and blinking hard, John aimed again. The weight of the armour and the lance made his arm burn with pain, but he kept it steady and kept the horse pounding forward without a moment's hesitation. His lance screeched against the shield, knocking Lancaster's man off balance. John swung the horse around to watch as his opponent clung to the saddle for a few paces, being tossed this way and that, before finally losing both his balance and his grip and falling heavily to the ground where he lay as still as death.

The cheering came loudly from one side of the lists and only grudgingly from where Lancaster's supporters were gathered. John hoisted what was left of his lance triumphantly as he galloped a victory circuit, passing the prone figure on the way. Then he threw the lance to the ground and went to see who it was he had killed. He slowed his horse to a trot as Lancaster's squires huddled around the body. As they carefully removed the helm, John saw the fair hair that he had ruffled so often and horror rose with the bile into his mouth. He flung himself from his horse and to his knees at the man's side.

'Eble!' he sobbed. 'Eble. Speak to me!'

★   ★   ★

At first Eble le Strange could not understand why he couldn't breathe. Neither could he understand why he was lying on what appeared to be a green bed nor why his friend, John de Warenne, had two faces.

'Speak to me!' pleaded John, but Eble was struggling for any breath to fill his lungs and was incapable of speech. Slowly he began to recall what had happened. He had been jousting and one of the Earl of Surrey's team had knocked him from his horse. He tried to raise a hand to reassure his friend, but it wouldn't move.

'Is he all right?' John was asking the squires who were now lifting him from the ground. He heard them ask his friend to move aside but was vaguely aware that John was walking beside him as they carried him back to a tent and laid him on a pallet.

He woke again as the stench of burning feathers assaulted him. He coughed but it was agony.

'Good,' said the barber surgeon, staring into his eyes. 'You're back with us. How many of me do you see?'

'One, you bastard — and that's one too many,' croaked Eble as he recalled that it was the surgeon's wrenching at his arm and the pain that followed which had caused him to relapse into oblivion.

'Your shoulder was loosened from its socket, but I've put everything back where it should be,' said the surgeon. 'You'll have to keep your arm closely bandaged to your body for a while, but you'll live. Here.' He forced a liquid between Eble's lips. 'Swallow!' he instructed and having no other option Eble allowed the bitter draft to trickle down his throat. 'That will ease your pain for a while.

I'll come and check on you later.'

'Will he be all right?' asked John's voice.

'He'll be fine,' replied the surgeon. He stood up and his place was taken by his anxious friend.

'I am so sorry,' said John. Eble feared he was about to grasp his sore shoulder but John remembered just in time and pulled his hand back. 'I had no idea that it was you. I would never have come at you so fiercely if I had.'

'And you used to be so afraid of the joust,' whispered Eble, every word an agonising effort. He felt as if he had been crushed beneath a pile of heavy stones, though the surgeon's medicine was already beginning to dull the edges of the pain and his grasp on reason.

'Lancaster did this deliberately. I'm sure of it!' said John and just before the blackness took him again Eble tried to nod in agreement.

★ ★ ★

'He set us against one another purposely,' repeated John. It was morning again and although Eble ached and throbbed he could now focus on his friend's face and make some sense of what he was saying.

John de Warenne had been allowed to visit

Eble where he lay on his bed in the corner of the men's chamber, but only after Lancaster had been to see him first, to express his disappointment in him. Lancaster had not said a word about his health or wished him well, but had remarked that he would probably not be fit for his duties for a long time, if ever, and that he might have to find him some other employment. To a bystander it could have sounded as if he cared, but Eble had known Thomas long enough to realise that it was a threat and that he would most likely be sent to some place where Lancaster hoped he would come to even more harm.

'Of course he did it deliberately,' said Eble, as he tried and failed to find a comfortable position in which to lie. 'Someone has told him that Alicia and I are lovers and he is punishing me for it.'

'Lovers?' asked John, dropping to the stool beside Eble and lowering his voice. 'Have you . . . ?'

'No. Of course not. Do you think of nothing else?' he asked as John's eyes gleamed. 'But this is a warning to leave Alicia alone.'

'And will you? Leave her alone?' asked John.

'I promised her that I would help her to leave him,' said Eble.

John stood up again and went to stare out through the narrow slit of window that faced north. He seemed deep in thought and Eble waited for him to speak.

'Do you have a plan?' he asked after a moment.

'Alicia owns a manor at Canford in Dorset that was her mother's and her grandmother's. I told her to go there and wait for me. I promised her that I would take her somewhere safe.' Eble paused. 'It seems so stupid now, but I didn't know what else to do. She was upset and I wanted to help her.'

'Then Lancaster does not keep her prisoner at Pickering?' asked John.

'Not a prisoner, no. But I do not know the man who has replaced me as the head of her household. If he is loyal to Lancaster he may refuse to accompany her to lands that do not belong to his lord. I wish I knew that she was safe,' he added as he remembered the anguish on her face as she had watched him bury the cat. She had wrapped it tenderly in a length of expensive cloth and insisted that they prayed the Pater Noster over its grave. Then she had wept as he filled the hole with earth and when it was finished she had put her hand out and grasped his wrist.

'You will come for me? To Canford?' she

had asked. 'You will help me, won't you Eble?'

She had not spoken to him of any feelings that she might have for him, but he hoped that his feelings were returned. And the way she had looked at him with her bright, tear-filled eyes had made him certain that she was as distraught by their separation as he was.

John came back to the bed and sat down again. 'You know that your horse and your armour are forfeit to me,' he said.

'I know,' said Eble. He was fond of the stallion that he had been riding and would be sorry to part with it, even though he knew his friend would treat it well. The armour, too, was a great loss. It was the value of many years' savings from his wages and he knew it would be a long time before he would be able to replace it. He had hoped that his friend would not take what was owed, but it seemed as if John meant to. 'If you have come to gloat then I would prefer you to leave.'

'I haven't come to gloat,' said John, sounding hurt. He reached out but Eble fended him away with his good hand. 'I have an idea.'

'What idea?' asked Eble. John had a look in his eye that Eble knew was often the prelude to some mischief. 'What are you thinking of?'

'I am wondering if Lancaster would release you into my household. Would you be agreeable?'

'You know damn' well that I would!' replied Eble as he attempted to sit up, but was forced back by the pain. 'Though I'm not sure what use I'll be.'

★ ★ ★

'So the man's horse and armour are not reward enough. You demand the man as well?' asked Lancaster, keeping his back to John and pretending to read some documents on the trestle. 'Well if you think I'm going to offer you a ransom for him you could not be more mistaken. I don't doubt for a moment that you've concocted this idea together to get money from me. Well, do I look so stupid? No. Take his horse and armour and let that be enough.'

'And what of Eble le Strange, my lord?'

'What of him? He's not much good to me — a crippled squire with neither horse nor harness. He can go back to Wales, or wherever it is he comes from.'

'Then you will not object if I offer him some employment in my own household?'

Lancaster turned with a mocking grin. 'So what they used to say about you two is true? I doubted it after you took up with Maud de Nerford, but perhaps you like your sword to be well honed on both edges.'

John clenched his fists but tried not to allow Lancaster the satisfaction of seeing his anger.

'Eble le Strange is my friend,' he replied. 'And you wanted me to kill him.'

Lancaster smirked. 'It was an inspired pairing. The two of you, unknown to one another, each facing a man he was determined to beat.' He laughed. 'It was the best jousting I've seen in years — and I would have rejoiced if either one of you had killed the other. But take him if you must have him. I'll be glad to see you both gone.'

'My lord,' replied John, with a curt nod of his head. Although he was seething with all manner of cutting replies he pressed his lips together because, although he had always vowed that he would make Thomas of Lancaster regret his treatment of him, he could at last see a way.

★ ★ ★

There were men in the council chamber at Clarendon who greeted John de Warenne as a friend and he was grateful for it. He had become alienated from the other earls during the long disputes about the king and his favourites, and too many older men continued to judge him for his grandfather's errors. But these younger knights, whom the king favoured, smiled at him and greeted him warmly. They were all united by their love of the king and their hatred for Thomas of Lancaster, and it felt good.

'We are taking wagers on whether Lancaster will come, or if he will plead some illness again,' grinned Hugh Audley, who was sitting with his booted feet up on the bench.

'Though it's not much of a wager,' remarked Roger Damory. 'I think it's a pretty safe bet that Lancaster won't show up.'

'Then that will prove he is a traitor and I shall say so openly in the parliament,' replied Audley. 'What do you think, Warenne?

'I consider the man a traitor and a fool,' replied John, eyeing the pile of coins on the table. 'I'm willing to bet that he will not come — but is there anyone willing to bet against me?'

'That,' said William Montacute, who was eating a huge pie, 'is the flaw in the plan. I doubt there's a man here who expects Lancaster to come, except possibly the king.'

'Edward is ever the optimist,' smiled Damory.

There was a flurry of activity in the

doorway and Montacute brushed the remains of the pie from his tunic and wiped his hands on his hose as Hugh Audley dropped his feet to the ground and stood up.

The men bowed as the king came in and Roger Damory went down on one knee and took Edward's hand. He kissed it, and his lips lingered. The king smiled down and made no move to pull his hand away.

'John!' said Edward. 'How was your journey?'

'Tolerable,' he replied, 'despite the weather.'

'There is, as yet, no sign of my cousin Lancaster,' said Edward, 'although he sends letters to say that he will come, and that he is keen for us to be reconciled.'

'He is a liar, then,' remarked John. 'I do not believe that he will come or that he seeks reconciliation. He gathers men around him and stays within the walls of his castle at Pontefract as if it is a separate kingdom.' He paused as he saw the flicker of hurt cross the king's face. He knew that Edward and his cousin had once been close friends and that despite their disagreements Edward still sought to be on better terms with Thomas, though the man seemed determined to continue to hurt him.

'He is a traitor, sire,' said Damory, releasing the king's hand but still kneeling.

John watched as the king drew the man to his feet, his hands lingering on his arms.

'I will not wage war on my cousin,' said Edward firmly. 'But if he does not come to the parliament I will write to him again, and express my displeasure at his continued absence.'

'Perhaps we can do more than that to gain his attention,' said Damory with a sly smile. He turned to John. 'I received your message,' he said, 'and what you said is true. Lancaster's wife is indeed living at Canford.'

'What is this that you plot?' asked Edward, moving towards a chair by the hearth and beckoning the men to gather around him. 'How can this help?'

'The Earl of Lancaster shows you contempt, your grace, by refusing to attend parliament,' explained Damory. 'He is a traitor and I will openly declare as much for all to hear. But his treatment of his wife, the daughter of your good friend and advisor, the late Earl of Lincoln, is worse. He sends her away whilst he cavorts with his mistresses at the castle that was her childhood home. How must she feel?'

'I, too, am greatly troubled by what has befallen Alicia de Lacy,' agreed the king. 'I would like to help her, but what can I do?' A moment of silence hung on the air as Damory and the others glanced at John and then Edward gave him a quizzical look. 'What of her?' he asked.

'I have a squire who was previously in the countess's household. His name is Eble le Strange,' replied John. 'He has promised the countess that he will help her to leave her husband. If I were to offer to take her into my custody I do not think she would be unwilling.' John paused as the king narrowed his eyes, the consequences of such an act forming in his mind.

'I will have no part of this,' he warned them. 'But neither will I prevent it. If the lady is amenable then you may give her shelter and I will not intervene to have her returned to her husband.'

'Thank you, your grace,' said John, unable to prevent a smile of satisfaction from settling on his face. Now, not only could he help the countess and his friend with the king's consent, he could show Thomas of Lancaster that he had gone too far in pitting him against Eble at the tournament.

★   ★   ★

Eble was waiting in the bedchamber that had been given to John for the duration of his visit. He had arranged a tub of hot water for his lord and was busy laying out clean linen. John was not keen on bathing, believing that it was dangerous, especially in the winter time when all manner of bad humours could enter the body through the skin. But Eble had infused the water in the tub with restorative herbs and he hoped that John would not argue or delay too long, as he was keen to use the tub himself once his friend was finished with it. He did not fear the dangers of washing and enjoyed the feel of the warm water on his skin. He had got into the habit of taking a regular bath when he had been at Pickering. It was something Alicia did and it was she who had scoffed at the supposed dangers, saying that she liked to smell fragrant and that she appreciated cleanliness in others.

Eble looked up as John came in. He seemed pleased and Eble hoped that it was because his enquiries about Alicia had resulted in some definite news.

'It is all arranged,' said John as he sat down in the steaming water and held out his hand for the cloth. He frowned as he rubbed beneath his armpits and Eble saw that he was determined not to remain in the tub for a moment longer than was necessary. 'The king wishes me to take the countess into my protection!'

Eble stared at him. 'You cannot do that!' he protested.

'Why not?'

'Because I promised her that I would help her to leave her husband, not that I would deliver her into your hands to be used as a pawn. This is not for the sake of Alicia. This is just so that you can be revenged on Lancaster!'

He fell silent as a man-at-arms knocked at the door. 'Is everything all right, my lord? I heard raised voices,' he said, looking suspiciously at Eble.

'Get out!' John told him, holding the cloth across his private parts until the man had gone. Then he reached for the linen towel that was warming before the fire and without asking Eble to assist him he stepped from the tub and began to towel himself dry.

'This makes no difference to your promise,' he said. 'Where would you have taken her anyway?'

'I was thinking of Shropshire.'

'And do you think your young nephew would welcome her?' asked John.

Eble frowned. His eldest brother had died only two years after their father and the castle at Knockin was under the control of his brother Hamon until their elder nephew came of age in October. He could see that taking Alicia there would not be ideal.

'You know what people will say,' he argued. 'They will say that you have abducted her so that you can make her your wife. They will say that you are trying to divorce Jeanne de Bar because you want to marry the Countess of Lancaster.'

'You know that isn't true. You know that I only want Maud. And I have no intention of harming the countess — in any way.'

Eble looked at his friend who was standing, draped in the towel. His hair was standing up in damp spikes and his face held an expression of hurt.

'Of course I know that you will not harm her,' he said. 'I am just telling you what people will say — and what they will believe. How can that help Alicia? Her circumstances are bad enough already. There are those who will claim that she is a willing victim. And some will say that she encouraged it, that she is a . . . whore.' He kicked a stool in a sudden show of anger. 'I do not want people to say those things about her,' he muttered.

John dropped the damp towel and reached for the clean undershirt that Eble had laid on the bed. There was a tense silence as he pulled it over his head. He had neglected to dry his back and the linen stuck to his skin as he struggled with it. Eble longed to go and help him, to take up the towel and dry him properly and help him with his clothing. But he folded his arms and glared at his friend.

'People are already saying those things,' said John when he had finally pulled his shirt straight and fastened his braies. 'I'm surprised you haven't heard them yourself. Though, of course, you were abed with all the sense knocked out of you at Pontefract, so perhaps you didn't hear the gossip that you and Alicia were lovers, which is why Lancaster wanted you killed in the joust.'

'You lie!' accused Eble.

'No. Believe me, it was true. I heard it myself. I'm sorry, Eble,' said John, 'but the reputation of the countess is tarnished already and there is nothing you can do to redeem it. Besides, how can you arrange this on your own? You will need my help.'

Eble continued to glare at the floor with his arms folded, but he knew that John was right. His vision of riding to rescue Alicia as if he were some gallant knight in a romance was appealing, but not practical. He would need armed men to ride with him and a cart so that she could bring her valuables with her. She might even want one or more of her ladies to accompany her; he knew that she was close to Edith. And the journey to Castle Reigate was not so far as the one to Knockin.

There would be more chance of reaching it safely.

'All right,' he said at last. 'We will do it your way.' John smiled at his capitulation and ruffled his hair as he bent to gather the wet towels and sheets ready for the laundress.

19

It was the Monday before Ascension Day and the tips of green leaves were bursting from the fat winter buds on the oak trees. Since my arrival at Canford I had remained indoors, inspecting linens, supervising the cleaning of the chambers, and waiting for Eble. But I had grown restless and as we took breakfast at the scrubbed trestle in the hall I asked William Fischer to see my horse saddled. I had decided to take my little merlin and go hunting.

I was soothed by the warmth of the sun on my back as we rode along. Edith had come with me, and two squires. The merlin was restless on my wrist. She could hear the birdsong all around and was eager for me to release her so that she might make a kill. When I let go of the jesses, she flew like a small but well aimed dagger as she sighted a song thrush and gave chase. As the men scanned the sky, following her progress, I felt a slight tug at my skirt and glanced down, thinking that it had snagged on a branch. The boy raised a finger to his lips and handed me a letter before disappearing into the trees as quickly as he had come. I stared after him not quite believing what had happened, but when I looked at the letter I saw the imprint of two leopards in the sealing wax and I was gripped with an excitement that scarcely allowed me to breath. The letter was from Eble.

Knowing that I could trust no one, except Edith, I pushed it into the purse that hung on my belt. I knew that I must not draw attention to anything unusual having happened. I did not trust the squires. So I looked up into the sky just in time to see the bird make its kill.

The day, which I had hoped to enjoy, seemed long, although as soon as the light began to fail we returned to the manor house. Once in my bedchamber, I sent Edith to fetch hot water, then, in the light of a candle, broke open the seal. My hands were trembling as I read the short message. I will come for you on the morrow — market day. Send your men away and fill a few coffers with whatever you will need. Be ready. Eble.

'Is anything wrong, my lady?' asked Edith when she returned with the jug. Guiltily I hid the letter behind my back, but then decided that I must tell her what it said because I needed her help. And I knew from our time together at Pickering that she liked and respected Eble, and that she hated my husband as much as I did.

'Can we send William Fischer and the squires on some errand to the market?' she asked when I had shown her the letter.

'Perhaps I can give them a holiday? There is a horse fair at the village tomorrow as well as the market and I daresay they will be keen enough to go. They have worked hard since we arrived and if I say it is to thank them they will not suspect.'

William Fischer was reluctant to leave us alone, but I reassured him that we were perfectly safe and that we intended to spend the day in the dairy making cheese and butter. In the end he agreed, persuaded by his own desire to see the horses that were for sale. I gave him a list of the things I pretended to need and soon after the sun had risen the men put on their cloaks and boots and were on their way. As soon as Edith and I had watched them leave we began to pack.

'I cannot take everything,' I said. 'I don't even know if Eble will bring anyone with him, or how big the wain will be.' I stared around the hall in despair, not knowing where to begin and how to decide what should go and what should be left behind.

'We must take everything of value,' said Edith, 'the cups and plates and the best linen cloths and bedding.' She began to pull coffers into the centre of the hall and lift the lids. 'Go up to the bedchamber and pack your clothes,' she told me. 'I will arrange things down here.'

'And the tapestry,' I said. 'We must not leave that behind.'

As I folded gowns and underlinen I forced myself to remain calm. There were so many things that could go wrong but fretting would achieve nothing. We paused for a dinner of bread and cheese, both of us too excited to eat much, and by early afternoon everything was ready. Then we waited and, as Edith watched from the window, I checked and re-checked the coffers to be sure that nothing of importance had been left out of them.

'Is there no sign?' I asked. 'It will grow dark soon and the men will return from the fair.'

'They will stay late to spend the money you gave them in the taverns,' said Edith. 'Do not fret. You will exhaust yourself with pacing up and down.'

'It is grown too late,' I said. 'He must have been delayed. I do not think he will come now.' I sat down on one of the coffers and began to wonder if we should unpack them again. If William Fischer saw them he would become suspicious and might send word to my husband.

'My lady! I can see horsemen coming!'

'It may not be Eble,' I said, still not

allowing myself to believe that he was really on his way. The sound of hoof beats and the groaning wheels of a wain came closer until they were in the courtyard. I stared at the door, wondering if some stranger would knock; perhaps someone seeking shelter for the night. Then the latch was lifted and the door opened quietly. Eble glanced inside.

'Is it safe? Is it all right?' he asked.

'You've come!'

'We must not delay,' he said. 'Is everything ready?' He glanced at the coffers and signalled to his men to come in and Edith hurried forward to show them what was to be carried out. 'Get your cloak,' he told me and watched as I pulled it around myself. 'Ready?'

'Yes,' I told him breathlessly.

'Let's go.'

Outside, in the twilight, the men were fastening the coffers onto the wain. Eble's capable hands took hold of me firmly around the waist and he lifted me up onto his horse as if I weighed nothing. I felt the saddle move slightly as he put his foot to the stirrup and mounted behind me. His chest pressed against my back as he leaned forward to gather the reins and as he urged the horse forward his arm settled around me, strong and warm and welcome. I allowed my weight to fall against him. I felt his breath on my cheek. I closed my eyes and for a moment allowed myself to be lost in the pleasure of the closeness of his body.

The darkness fell quickly as we took the track that led away from Canford Manor. The air rushed past my face as Eble urged the horse on. I tried to tell him how happy I was, but the wind whisked my words away as Eble loosened his grip on me for a moment to raise my hood and drape it over my face so that I could not be seen.

20

Each morning that I woke at Castle Reigate I gave thanks that my husband could not hurt me. I was safe from him. John de Warenne had provided a generous chamber for me and I wanted for nothing.

Eble was often in my company. I liked to watch him. I watched his fingers when we played chess. I watched him push his hands through his hair when he was deep in thought. I watched him as he rode beside me when we went out to hunt. When he touched me, to help me on or off the little bay mare that John de Warenne had given me to ride, I was troubled. Part of me wanted to know him more intimately, but part of me was afraid, and I could not find the right words to explain how I felt.

When he went north to escort Maud de Nerford from Pontefract, I missed him so much that the ache was physical. Edith brewed tinctures for me to drink but nothing made me feel better until I woke one morning and sensed that he was coming back. And sure enough, that afternoon, the horns sounded to announce his imminent arrival and I went to watch from the wall walk.

As the small party rode into the bailey, John de Warenne hurried forward to lift the woman down from her horse. He put his arms around her and kissed her. Then, one by one, he lifted down two small boys, well wrapped in warm cloaks. He hugged and kissed them as well and then put his arms around Maud de Nerford again.

I went down the spiral steps to greet them and when I reached the hall, they were coming up the outer stairway. The little boys were dragging their feet and Eble picked up the smaller one and carried him in. The child looked pale-faced and exhausted and the older one seemed bewildered as he stared around, holding tightly onto his mother's hand. Maud de Nerford was more reserved than I had expected, but very pretty with an appealing smile and big eyes. She curtseyed to me and I kissed her cold cheeks and said that I was pleased to meet her at last.

I helped to unwrap the little boys and wash their hands. We fed them, although they were both on the verge of sleep, and Edith took them off to their beds. Then, when we had eaten and were seated at the hearth, Eble told us how he had found Maud — and John's face grew grim with anger as she recounted how Lancaster's men had forced them from their home. I think I was the one who was least surprised at my husband's cruelty and I reached for Maud's hand and held it tightly as she spoke.

Before long I could see that she was tearful with her tiredness and I suggested that she go to bed. John went with her and Eble and I were left alone with half empty cups in our hands and only one another and the embers of the fire for company.

'I thank God you found her,' I said after a moment. 'What my husband did was unforgiveable.'

'You know that I have no good words to say about him,' replied Eble.

'They seem to be very much in love,' I said.

'Yes.' He followed my gaze towards the door where John and Maud had gone hand in hand to his chamber on the upper floor. 'He used to say that there was no such thing as love, but I always warned him that one day he would be proved wrong.'

'It is a pity that Thomas was so stubborn in the matter of his divorce. These marriages that are arranged by parents and guardians can be a curse.'

'Do you think your husband will seek to divorce you?' asked Eble after a moment's silence. He was playing with the cup in his hands and glanced away, towards the fire, when I looked at him.

'I don't know. But when he has made such strenuous arguments against the ending of John's marriage I do not see how he could justify divorcing me. Besides, he has women enough and he will not risk losing anything of mine that he regards as his own. The only thing I have not given him is a legitimate son — and I am glad. I wanted children. But if I had borne them he would have taken them away from me — just like everything else.'

The logs settled with a sigh in the hearth. It was growing dark outside and I knew that soon it would be time to go to my own bedchamber. Whilst Eble had been away I had missed his physical presence acutely and, even though I knew that it would be a sin, I could no longer deny that I was ready to discover what the act that had always been so sordid with my husband would feel like with him.

I reached out my hand to cover his as it lay on his knee. 'We have been friends for a long time . . . ' I began.

'And our friendship is precious to me,' he said. 'If friendship is all you desire, my lady, then I will not press you to favour me with more. I am sorry if you — '

'Do not apologise to me,' I interrupted him. 'You have always been loyal to me — as my squire and as my friend. But . . . '

'But that is all I am to you, your squire, a man who is not even a knight.' He pulled his hand from beneath mine.

'No, Eble. You are much more to me than that.' I slipped from the bench onto my knees beside him and laid a hand on his thigh. It was warm and the muscles felt hard under my palm. 'If you knew what my husband had done to me, how he had treated me, you would know why I have been reluctant,' I confessed. 'I am beset by unpleasant memories.'

'Alicia,' he said. 'I am as different from Thomas of Lancaster as day is from night.'

Slowly he cupped my face in the palms of his warm hands and bent his head towards me. I tensed and fought the urge to pull back, but he did not force his tongue into my mouth as Thomas would have done, but gently caressed my lips with his for a moment before releasing me. 'Will you come to my bed?' he asked.

'Come to mine,' I replied.

He took my hand and we left the cups and platters for the servants to clear away as we climbed the steps to my chamber.

His blue eyes studied me and I looked again at the breadth of his chest under his tunic and thought about how strong he had felt when I sat on the horse with him. I held out my hands to him and he came across the chamber and grasped them in his, lifting each one in turn to his lips to kiss it.

'My lady. Alicia. You are the most precious thing in the world to me,' he said. 'I have waited for you for so long. I . . . ' he hesitated.

'What is it?' I asked, sensing that there was something that was troubling him. Perhaps it worried him that what we were about to do was a sin. 'Eble?' I said, taking a hand from his and touching his face, feeling the mixture of roughness and softness on his cheek. He raised his own hand again and pressed my palm to his lips and closed his eyes. When he opened them he watched me with a look that made me feel wanted in a way I had never known before.

'I have loved you since I was a boy,' he said. 'I have loved you so much that I have never wanted another . . . never had another . . . '

It was a moment before I comprehended his meaning. My husband had defouled many women. He had lain with whores and prostitutes and village girls by the dozen — both before and after our marriage. I knew that Eble had never joined the other squires in the narrow lanes behind the taverns when he lived at Pontefract. And I knew that people said it was because he was in thrall to John de

Warenne and that women held no interest for him. He had had no woman whilst we were at Pickering — at least not one that I was aware of — but I had never thought that he had kept himself for me alone.

'Eble.' I gazed up at him in wonderment and traced the contours of his cheek and chin with my hand. I touched his hair then pressed my palm to the back of his neck and stretched up to kiss his lips with mine. They were warm and soft and he returned my kiss with eager anticipation.

As we moved apart I found that I was crying.

'What's wrong?' he asked.

'It is more than I deserve,' I said. 'You should not have denied yourself for me.'

'I wanted no other — only you,' he said as he bent to renew his kiss. 'But you must forgive me,' he said, drawing away again after a moment.

'For what?' I asked as I put my arms around his waist and held him against me, feeling the power and the strength of his body.

'I may not know the best ways to please you,' he said.

'Eble,' I whispered. 'You could not have pleased me more. As for the rest. Do not worry.' I ran my hands up and down his back, feeling the muscles of his shoulders. He put his arms around me, holding me close and his hands echoed my movements. Then I pushed him gently from me and reached to grasp his tunic. He was too tall for me to lift it over his head, and he laughed softly as I stood on tiptoe and struggled. Then he pulled it off and his undershirt as well and I ran my hands over the warmth of his body, feeling the softness of the fair hair that grew in the centre of his chest. I kissed the freckles that dusted his shoulders. Then he pulled me tightly against him again and wrapped me in his arms and my fear dissolved into longing as he kissed my face and caressed my body with his hands.

At last I pulled away, breathless and smiling, to unpin the wimple that covered my hair.

'Will you help me?' I asked, fumbling with my braids.

Eble stretched out his bare arms and I bent my head towards him until I felt my hair tumble loose around my shoulders as he ran his fingers through it. Then he reached for the fastening on my gown and I watched his face fill with wonder as he drew off my clothing and saw my body beneath. Naked, I lay down on the bed and he leant over me and kissed me.

'Take these off,' I said as my fingers

fumbled with the drawstring on his braies. 'I want to see you as well.'

My husband had never revealed himself to me. Whenever he had used me it had been brutal and he had not lingered. I had caught glimpses as he hurriedly pushed himself back inside his clothing but nothing more. Now I watched as Eble stepped out of his underlinen beside the bed and I reached out a hand to touch him. He groaned and clasped his fingers over mine, holding them there. 'Come and lie down,' I said and when he did I knelt astride him and when I bent to kiss his lips my breasts brushed over his chest and his warm hands ran down the length of my back and clasped me against him. After a while I pushed his hands away and raising myself slightly I took him in my hand and guided him to my secret place. He was hesitant at first and I was the one who pressed my body down over his, gently taking him inside me with each slow and careful movement until we relaxed and for the first time I felt pleasure not pain in the intimate touch as we moved together.

I could not believe that this was the same act that I had endured with my husband. I felt as if I was floating through the air like music and my body sang in harmony with his and the song was one of joy.

21

'No!' Edward exploded. 'I do not want it!'

'We don't care what you want!' Thomas of Lancaster shouted back across the chapter house of the minster at York where the parliament was being held. 'You agreed to be constrained by the ordinances and reign by the counsel of your magnates! Don't you recall that we signed a treaty at Loughborough, and that you exchanged the kiss of peace with me — and that you even gave me the gift of a horse? Which has gone lame, by the way!'

The air quivered with anger and resentment as the two men glared at each other.

'Your Grace,' interrupted the Earl of Pembroke in a more conciliatory tone. 'I think it is for the best if Roger Damory is removed and we appoint Hugh le Despenser as your chamberlain and Bartholomew Badlesmere as your steward.'

'But I have the right to appoint my own steward!' argued the king.

'Your Grace, I must insist that you follow our advice in this matter,' replied Pembroke, managing to sound both reasonable and adamant in the same breath.

John de Warenne watched as the king's expression took on the look of a petulant child.

'But I am the king!' he said.

Lancaster snorted in derision. Pembroke glared at him and John de Warenne seethed. Even though Edward had told Lancaster to desist from taking John's lands, he had gone on to attack the Warenne holdings in Shropshire and Wales. John had still not regained control of his Yorkshire castles and he was burning with resentment at being forced to pay compensation for the kidnap of Alicia, even though Thomas had not so much as exchanged a letter with his wife or asked for her to be returned to him.

'Your Grace,' said Pembroke to the king. 'I must insist that you agree to this.' He nodded to the scribe to dip a quill into the ink, but Edward continued to stare at him in open defiance until, finally, he snatched it and scrawled his signature across the parchment.

★ ★ ★

When Eble received the letter from his nephew he was faced with a dilemma. If he were to help defend the family lands from the grasp of Hugh le Despenser then it would mean aligning himself with Thomas of Lancaster, and the thought of that made him sick to the pit of his stomach. But his nephew wrote that he feared for the land at Knockin — and Eble could not deny that Hugh le Despenser, the king's chamberlain, was becoming increasingly greedy and dangerous. And land was power.

Having risen from a political nobody with only a few impoverished manors, Despenser had inherited Glamorgan after the death of his wife's brother at Bannockburn, but discontent with that the man had complained that John Mowbray had taken possession of Gower from his father-in-law illegally, even though the transfer of marcher lands required no royal licence. The king had confiscated Gower and it was clear that he intended to give it to Despenser. The marcher lords were furious. It was a blatant attack on them and Eble's nephew was afraid that his own recent inheritance of Knockin might be the next target.

With the letter folded in his hand he went to look for John de Warenne. He was down at the lists, watching some new horses being put through their paces and Eble went to stand beside him as he leaned on a fence.

'That grey looks promising,' said John with a nod of his head. 'What do you think of him?'

Eble watched as the rider turned the horse and urged him forwards, leaning to aim a blunted lance at the loop on a post. The horse's stride was steady and long. He was eager yet seemed responsive to the commands.

'He seems well trained.'

'I bought him at the fair yesterday,' said John. 'I thought it was time you had a decent destrier. Perhaps you could ride him against me in a re-match. You might stand some slight chance,' he joked. 'Do you not like him?' he asked as the horse cantered past and Eble remained silent.

'Yes . . . he's an impressive animal,' said Eble. 'But I did not seek you out to discuss the horses.'

'What then?' asked his friend with a shrewd look.

'A letter has come from my nephew. He is worried about the castle at Knockin and he has asked me to go home for a while.'

John turned from the horses and gave Eble his full attention. 'In what way is he worried?' he asked. 'Trouble with the Welsh?'

Eble shook his head. 'No. Trouble with Hugh le Despenser,' he said.

'Pembroke was mistaken when he suggested him for chamberlain,' said John when Eble had shown him the letter.

'My nephew has agreed to go to a meeting of marcher lords at Pontefract,' said Eble.

'Pontefract! Good God, Eble! You cannot mean to go there!'

'What choice do I have?' he asked. 'I cannot stand by and see him lose everything — all that my father and my brothers worked for. He may be the heir, but he is only twenty-one. I cannot let him down.'

'I see your point. But going to Pontefract means taking sides with Thomas of Lancaster against the king. What do you think Alicia will say? I take it you have not spoken to her on the subject?'

'I thought to hear your opinion first.'

'What do you want me to say?' asked John. 'Should I forbid you to go? Or send you with my blessing to join the ranks of a man we both hate and whose wife has willingly put herself into my care?'

Eble pushed the letter inside his tunic and stared at the grey horse as it was led across to them for a closer inspection.

'I supposed I thought you might help me decide what to do.'

'Look at me and tell me that you have not already made your decision,' challenged John.

'Will you take care of Alicia whilst I am gone?' asked Eble, meeting his friend's eye. 'And whatever the outcome do not let her fall into her husband's hands.'

'You have my word,' he said. Then he grasped the reins of the grey and handed them to Eble. 'And take this horse,' he said. 'You will probably need him.'

'You cannot mean to join my husband!' Alicia was sitting on the window seat. She had greeted Eble with a serene and beautiful smile when he had joined her, but now that he had explained his intention she fixed him with a look of intense displeasure. 'You cannot do that!' she told him.

'But, Alicia — ' He fell silent as she held up her hand.

'No! There is nothing you can say that will make any difference. I cannot believe that you would betray me like this,' she told him.

'Alicia!' he protested as he tried to take her hand in his. 'I have said that I will go with my nephew to Pontefract. That is all.' She pulled her hand away and stood up, turning her back on him to stare down into the courtyard. 'My nephew is very young,' he explained, 'and if I do nothing he will take the Knockin contingent to Lancaster anyway. It is better that I should go and try to persuade him not to.'

'But Thomas has tried to have you killed once. Don't you think he will try again?'

'His argument is with John de Warenne, not with me.'

'His argument is with you as well Eble. It is no secret that you are my lover. Do you think he will welcome a man who has cuckolded him? His pride will not let him.'

'Thomas of Lancaster will need all the support he can muster if he is to lead a rebellion against the king.'

'A rebellion against the king? Will it come to that?' she asked, turning back to him.

'Your husband has always had his eye on the throne. This discontent that is sown by Despenser will only drive more men to support him.'

'And if he should become king?' she asked. 'What will I do if you are not here to protect me?' Her eyes began to brim with tears and Eble went to her but she moved away from him.

'John de Warenne will protect you,' he said.

'Will he?' she asked. 'Or will he also abandon me if it should suit his purpose?'

'Alicia, I am not abandoning you.'

'Are you sure?' she demanded, with anger glinting like fire in her dark eyes. 'You men are all the same! You think women are to be used — and nothing more!'

'Alicia!' He grasped her by the arms, sorely tempted to shake some good sense into her.

'Go on then!' she challenged him. 'Do what

my husband would do, depending on his mood. Will you slap me? Or will you force yourself on me?'

Eble released her as if she were burning hot. 'You know that I would do neither. You insult me by comparing me with him,' he told her as he watched her rub her arms and glare at him. He felt guilty that he had grasped her so hard and yet there was a part of him that would have enjoyed subduing her. Even now, when they made love he allowed her to initiate and control it, but there was a growing desire in him to take that dominance from her.

'I'm sorry,' he muttered. 'But I am left with little choice. My nephew needs me and I have a duty to go to him.'

'What about your duty to me? I thought you were my squire?'

'No longer, my lady. John de Warenne is my lord since your husband dismissed me from his household — and he has given me his permission to leave.'

'I thought that I could trust you,' she chastised him. 'But it seems that I was mistaken.'

'Alicia, please do not make this harder for us than it needs to be,' he pleaded.

'I thought you loved me!'

'Alicia, I do love you. But I cannot stand by

and do nothing if Hugh le Despenser takes my family lands.'

'Go then,' she said, waving him away with her hands.

'Alicia — '

'Just go!' she shouted as the tears began to roll down her cheeks.

Defeated, Eble left her, only glancing back to see her crumple, like a doll stuffed with rags, onto the window seat.

He paused half way down the steps that led from the chamber and was tempted to go back and try to make her see reason — try to make her understand that no matter how much he loved her he could not stand by and do nothing as the lands that had been his father's and his grandfather's were snatched away on some whim of the king's. But he knew how stubborn she could be and how reluctant to admit that she was ever in the wrong. If he went back he might only make matters worse. He was tempted to thrust his head against the wall so that the pain that would ensue might dull the agony that ripped through him.

'Damn! Damn! Damn!' he swore and glared at the passing servant who stared at him in alarm.

22

Although Knockin had not changed it was so long since Eble had been home that it looked unfamiliar as he approached it. The grey had proved its worth. It was still eager despite the speed of the journey and Eble urged it on to reach the safety of the castle walls.

The echoes from the iron shoes on the horse's feet rang out across the small courtyard and, as a groom came to take the reins, Eble saw the door to the hall at the top of the steps was open and his nephews, John and Roger, were looking out for him. He waved a greeting and would have run up the stairs two at a time had he not been so stiff from the hours in the saddle.

'Welcome!' John greeted him as he stepped into the warm hall which seemed to have shrunk in his absence. Eble hugged both him and his younger nephew before casting an enquiring look towards the stranger by the fire.

'This is my uncle,' his nephew told the man as he stood up. Then he drew Eble forwards. 'I do not think you have met Roger Mortimer,' he said.

Eble took the man's outstretched hand. He knew Mortimer by reputation if not by sight. He had served as King's Lieutenant and Justiciar in Ireland and been a loyal supporter of Edward, though gossip abounded that he had left the court because of his hatred of Hugh le Despenser.

'I'm pleased to meet you,' said Eble.

'And I am pleased that you have chosen to support your family,' he replied. 'We live in uncertain times and every man must guard against the loss of his lands. Your nephew tells me that you are a squire of the Earl of Surrey.'

'Yes, my lord. Though formerly I was in the household of the Earl of Lancaster, but there was some trouble . . . '

'Yes. The countess,' said Mortimer, looking closely at him. 'I have heard that she favours you. What does she say about your coming here?'

'She is very angry,' replied Eble, the memory of Alicia's tearful face still troubling him. 'Angry that I ally myself with her husband.'

'It is a time for strange bedfellows,' said Mortimer. 'And if it comes to a choice between Lancaster and the king there are many who will abandon Edward because of Despenser. The king does himself no favours to allow that man to rule him so closely.'

'I would support any man who will help to safeguard these lands,' said Eble as he took off his cloak and accepted a drink. 'I will not stand by and see them given to Despenser on some pretext.'

'The other marcher lords would agree with you,' said Mortimer. 'I hear that you are to go to Pontefract?'

'I will accompany my nephew, at his request,' replied Eble, glancing at John who was taking no part in the conversation but was listening intently to what the older men had to say. 'Although I cannot say that I am looking forward to it. Will you join us?'

Mortimer shook his head. 'I am not yet ready to take sides with Lancaster. But that does not rule out action against Despenser,' he said. 'The man must be stopped. There is no question about that.'

★   ★   ★

'There is a long history of enmity between Mortimer and Hugh le Despenser,' said Roger as they watched him ride away the next morning.

'I know,' said Eble. 'It goes back to the battle of Evesham when Mortimer's grandfather killed Despenser's grandfather. Men rarely let the past lie,' he said, thinking of John de Warenne and the way he was still held responsible for his grandfather's shortcomings.

'Mortimer plans to call a council of marcher lords,' said John.

'And will you go?'

'I will go to Pontefract first. Lancaster wields more power. But if he will not act then I will do whatever is necessary.'

'And I am here to help. You can depend on that,' said Eble.

★ ★ ★

As the towers of Pontefract castle became visible on the horizon Eble felt his heart beat faster. It was one thing to speak of a matter, but quite another to do it. Even if he was quiet and kept his head low, he did not think that his presence would go unnoticed and he was afraid of what might happen. Perhaps Alicia had been right. It was foolhardy. But he had little choice and he hoped that a common enemy might prevent Lancaster from taking revenge on him.

He led his two young nephews through the gates and to the stables where others were already gathering despite the king's order not to hold any assemblies. This one was only lightly disguised as a tournament and Eble doubted that there would be much jousting on the frozen lists.

Once the horses had been attended to they went inside to warm their hands at a brazier and find a place for their pallets that was not in a draught. But the best places had already been taken and they had to unroll their beds in a corner under a window, well away from the fires. It would be a cold night, thought Eble, as a servant greeted him cordially and he knew that news of his arrival would be quickly relayed to the earl.

At supper time he found himself at the same table, well down the hall, where he had been seated on his first day and his feelings of disquiet were similar, except that it was not the benevolent Henry de Lacy who took his place at the top table, but Thomas, Earl of Lancaster.

Later, as men broke up into groups to discuss Despenser he made his way out to the latrine and found his way blocked.

'You have some gall, to show up here, Welsh boy,' said Lancaster. 'How is your shoulder?'

'As good as new, thank you, my lord,' he replied.

'Will you be jousting then?'

'I think I will leave that to my nephews.'

'Afraid to lose?'

'Not at all,' said Eble trying to sound more confident than he felt.

'It makes me tempted to issue a challenge to you myself. After all, we still have a score to settle. How is my wife, by the way? Are you enjoying her company?'

'The countess was in good health when I left Castle Reigate.'

'She's a frigid witch. You're welcome to her,' said Lancaster. 'Or is she still toying with you? Like a cat with a mouse?' He swayed slightly and put out a hand to steady himself against the archway. 'Or do you sleep with John de Warenne?'

Eble balled his hand into a fist and glanced around. But there were too many witnesses. He would not spend a night in the dungeon for the sake of knocking Lancaster's teeth down his throat.

'Excuse me,' he muttered and pushed past as Lancaster staggered and regained his balance.

'Don't blame me!' he called after Eble. 'I showed her what a real man could do for her, so it's no wonder she doesn't warm to a sod like you!'

★　★　★

Eble seethed with anger all night long, turning over and over on his pallet and earning the curses of those who were trying to sleep nearby. He cursed himself for allowing Thomas of Lancaster to rile him and as he lay awake he consoled himself by imagining how it would have felt to knock him to floor. By morning his head and his body ached and he was so tired he found it hard to concentrate on the arguments and discussions that raged to and fro about what should be done. The barons were in agreement that Despenser must be stopped and had already half-hatched a plan to invade his lands and take back what they considered to be rightfully theirs. Lancaster agreed in principle but, typically of him, was reluctant to take any part. In the end it was decided that he should form the figurehead and that the marcher lords would take action against Despenser with his blessing.

It was with relief that Eble rode away from Pontefract a few days later. Even though it seemed that he would be forced to fight on Lancaster's behalf he was glad to put as much physical distance between himself and the earl as possible.

'You are quiet,' said his nephew as they rode west towards the marches. 'I hope you don't regret coming home.'

'It is not without its difficulties,' said Eble. 'But no. I have no regrets. I have not forgotten our family motto. Mihi Parta Tueri. I will fight for what is mine.'

★ ★ ★

They had not been back at Knockin long before a messenger came and summoned them to another meeting, called by Roger Mortimer at his uncle's castle at Chirk. Grim faced marcher lords settled themselves in the hall, jostling for the best places nearest the fire to warm themselves from the icy roads outside. Amongst them Eble recognised the faces of Hugh Audley and Roger Damory — men who had once been close to the king but whose place in Edward's affections had been taken by Despenser.

It was with nods of agreement and murmurs of assent that they listened to Mortimer tell them that Despenser must be pursued, laid low and utterly destroyed.

'The king has come to Gloucester and orders us to attend on him there. What should we do?' asked one man.

'You are free to go if you choose,' said Mortimer. 'But can you be assured of your safety if you go into the presence of Despenser?' The hum of conversation increased as men turned to one another to discuss what they should do. 'I have sent a message to the king,' continued Mortimer, 'and told him that I fear for my life if Despenser is present and so I will not attend.'

'Despenser is welded to the king like a barnacle to the bottom of a ship,' remarked someone and there were snorts of laughter and comments about the nature of the relationship between the two men. Eble felt uncomfortable. He had heard such things hinted at about himself and John de Warenne and he was reluctant to give them credence. But whether Despenser slept in the king's bed or not it was true that he was rarely far from his side and wherever the king went you would find Hugh le Despenser wielding his authority and making some extra money by demanding bribes from those who desired to speak with the king.

'Perhaps Edward would agree to Despenser being put into the custody of the Earl of Lancaster until he can be brought before parliament to answer the charges against him,' suggested someone. There was a hoot of derision.

'After what he did to Gaveston? The king will hardly agree to that!'

'Then what is to be done?'

Eble waited as the silence in the hall grew tense.

'When diplomacy has been exhausted, there is only force left,' said Roger Mortimer, quietly. 'I propose we take up arms against Hugh le Despenser.'

★ ★ ★

Eble watched the line that stretched as far as he could see. He estimated that it must number around ten thousand men on foot and another eight hundred men-at-arms on horseback. In the distance, near to where Mortimer headed the column, he could see the king's banner fluttering in the spring sunshine. They rode on behalf of the realm, Mortimer had told them, though Eble doubted whether the king would agree.

Beside him his young nephews looked young and eager, both wanting to show off the skills they had learnt at the joust in more serious combat. But as they approached the walls of Newport, Eble saw that there were no bowmen lined up on the wall walk and the constable came out at Mortimer's command and handed over the keys without a fight. The garrison was far outnumbered and although the men had sworn fealty to Despenser it seemed that their allegiance did not stretch to dying for him.

Over the course of the next week they took

Despenser's castles at Cardiff and Caerphilly. The Welshmen were inclined to acquiesce to Mortimer's demands. They had no fondness for Hugh le Despenser and willingly swore on a copy of the Holy Gospel that they renounced his lordship over them and that they would stay loyal to the king in all things. And those less willing were persuaded by a night in the dungeon.

* * *

The king looked worried, thought John de Warenne, as he was ushered into the privy chamber. Edward kept glancing towards Hugh le Despenser who sat at the table with his arms tightly folded across his chest and fury lurking in his eyes.

'We should burn and loot their castles,' Despenser told the assembled group of barons and advisors. 'That will distract their attention from destroying what is rightfully mine. Do you know that they have hanged my men? Sir John Iwayn, Philip le Keu and Matthew de Gorges. All killed for defending my castles.' He pulled one hand free to strike it hard against the trestle. 'We will not allow this to go unpunished!'

'My lord,' said John. 'Much as I can sympathise with you on the loss of your castles, I think we need to tread carefully. It would be risky to provoke a war within the kingdom that might lay ruin to everything.'

'The king must rule with a firm hand!' shouted Despenser, leaning forward to glare at John across the table. 'Just because you will not challenge Lancaster for the return of your castles does not mean we should all be so weak-willed! I advise the king to show these rebels and traitors that they cannot take what is not theirs and go unpunished!'

There was a slight clearing of a throat in the silence that followed and John watched a messenger come forward with a letter for the king. Edward indicated that his clerk should open and read it.

'The rebels have met with the Earl of Lancaster in Yorkshire, Your Grace,' said the man. 'They have sworn to remove Despenser for good — and are marching south towards London.'

★ ★ ★

Mortimer and his army approached London towards the end of July. They were seen approaching the city gates — armed and with their banners unfurled in open challenge. And as more news trickled in, John learned that all the lands of both Hugh le Despenser and his father had been seized and laid waste — livestock stolen, crops burned. Mortimer had even entered the abbey at Stanleye and taken money and charters that Despenser had lodged with the monks for safe-keeping.

Was Eble out there with them, wondered John, as he paused at the top of the steps of the city wall and watched the Contrariants as they planted their banners and pitched their tents. He gazed down knowing that it was stupid to look, that there was no chance of recognising a man's face at this distance. But he prayed to God that his friend was safe, for Alicia's sake as well as his own. After Eble had left Reigate she kept to her own chamber and would speak to no one but her maid. Not even Maud could give her any comfort and he himself, uncomfortable in the presence of weeping women, had kept his distance although if there had been anything practical he could have done to ease her pain then he would have done it.

John heard heavy breathing and the Earl of Pembroke joined him, rubbing at the pain in his knee.

'What do you know of Mortimer?' he asked with a nod towards the gathering crowd below.

'Not much, except that he has always been loyal to the king, until now.'

'I rue the day I ever suggested Despenser's name as king's chamberlain,' muttered Pembroke. 'Who would have thought it would come to this?'

'It would be a wise man who could see into the future,' said John. 'Do you suppose they will demand Despenser's head?'

'They will demand his exile at the very least,' said Pembroke. 'And I'll not argue with that. But it will be harder to convince the king.'

'Indeed,' agreed John, thinking of the loving way that Edward's eyes followed Hugh's every move around his chamber. It would take more than a force of men at the city gates to persuade him to send his friend away for good.

'The king has asked me to meet with the rebel leaders at Clerkenwell,' said Pembroke. 'I would like you to come with me, to watch my back, if you are willing.'

'I owe you that much, at least,' said John as they turned away from the scene below.

Later that day, they were waiting in the parlour of Prior Thomas for Mortimer to arrive when a messenger was shown in. 'Despenser must go into exile. Nothing less is acceptable to us,' he told them.

'And if the king does not comply?' inquired Pembroke as he studied the man before him.

241

'Then we will burn the city,' he replied.

'Do you think they are serious?' asked John after the messenger had been shown out.

'I believe they are.'

'What shall we do?'

'We must persuade the king to do as they ask. Despenser must go.'

★ ★ ★

'No!' said Edward when they had been shown into his privy chamber and given an account of the terms that Mortimer had laid down.

'But my lord,' said Pembroke, 'why risk losing your kingdom for the sake of another? And remember the oath you swore at your coronation that you would listen to your barons, to enable you to reign in power and glory. Listen to us now and do not risk the loss of your kingdom.'

'No!' repeated Edward. He was adamant and would not be persuaded or cajoled into seeing reason or changing his mind. In the end he lost his temper and ordered them out of the chamber.

John found Lady de Vescy waiting near the door. She was biting her lip and looked guilty.

'The queen sent me to listen at the door to see what I can discover,' she explained. 'She

242

complains that she is told nothing since Hugh le Despenser was appointed to the king's chamber. Will he be exiled as the Contrariants are demanding?' she asked.

John beckoned her to walk with him and they made their way across the enclosed courtyard towards the queen's apartments.

'He will not listen,' he complained.

'It does not surprise me. His stubborn nature is not unknown to me,' she said. 'Would you like me to speak to him?'

'I will try anything that might influence him. The army at the gates will not disappear no matter how much Edward wishes it. If he will not agree to their demands I do not doubt that they will make good their threat to burn London.'

'I will ask him,' said the queen when John had given her the news. 'I will go down on my knees and beg him if that is what it takes to be rid of that man!'

John watched as she quivered with indignation. What on earth did the king see in Hugh le Despenser when he had a wife like this, he wondered. Queen Isabella was beautiful. Unlike Maud she was fair haired and her eyes were intensely blue under her neatly arched brows. The bodice of her gown was tightly fitted and above the half-moons of her breasts the pale skin was unblemished by a single freckle. Her only flaw, visible as she raised a hand, was a scar, a remnant from the night ten years ago when the pavilion in which she and the king had been sleeping had caught fire. If the king did not enjoy taking her to his bed then he was a fool, thought John. Had she not been the queen he would not have hesitated to work his own charm on her.

'Would you do that?' he asked. 'Would you beg the king?'

'You cannot ask such a thing of the queen,' said Lady de Vescy.

'Wait,' said John, holding up a hand to silence her. 'We must try everything.' He turned back to Isabella. 'Are you truly willing, my lady?' he asked.

★　★　★

Lady de Vescy accompanied Queen Isabella to the king. The hall was filled with barons and nobles still trying to persuade Edward to agree terms with the Contrariants. They and the scribes and clerks fell silent and bowed their heads as the queen walked to where her husband was seated on the dais.

Edward watched his wife as she approached him. Then she fell to her knees in front of him. 'Sire,' she begged, her hands clasped like a supplicant. 'I beg you. For my sake and for the sake of our children and for the sake of this realm, I beg you to agree to the exile of Sir Hugh le Despenser.'

There was an uncomfortable silence as the queen lowered her head and remained on her knees before the king. Many men averted their eyes at her humbling of herself. But it was a powerful plea and the king could do no other than to reach out to raise her to her feet and agree to what she desired.

23

The queen had the look of a conspirator, thought Lady de Vescy, when Isabella returned from the king's bedchamber. Since Jeanne de Bar had returned to France, Lady de Vescy had become the queen's closest confidante and it pleased her that the relationship between Edward and Isabella had improved since the exile of Hugh le Despenser. It was a wife's right to enjoy her husband's bed and lately Isabella had even hinted that she might, at last, be coming to love her husband.

'I am to go on a pilgrimage to Canterbury,' said the queen, 'and I am to return to London by way of Leeds Castle.'

'Leeds Castle? That is not the usual route from Canterbury to London,' said Lady de Vescy watching the young queen walk backwards and forwards with her eyes shining. She was like a child who had discovered some secret and was hugging it to her yet at the same time desperate for it to be discovered and shared. 'Besides, Leeds Castle belongs to Bartholomew Badlesmere,' she went on. The king's household steward had been sent to Pontefract to spy on Thomas of Lancaster and the marcher lords but, rather than returning with information he had chosen to join their cause, to the intense anger and frustration of Edward. 'What are you planning?' she asked.

'I am to ask for a night's lodging,' explained Isabella. 'Badlesmere's wife is in residence and my husband believes that she will refuse!'

'It would be a great insult to you if she were to do so,' remarked Lady de Vescy.

'Exactly!' replied Isabella. 'If she were to refuse me, then the king would have no choice but take action against her for so grave an insult! Will you help me to pack?' she asked.

'Of course,' said Lady de Vescy, although her thoughts were not on gowns and offerings for the shrine at the cathedral, but on the implications of Lady Badlesmere's refusal to admit the queen to her castle.

As Lady de Vescy prayed at the shrine of Thomas a Becket she contemplated the irony of what Edward had asked the queen to do. A pilgrimage to the shrine of a saint who had dared to question the authority of a king was to be followed by a plot to punish a Contrariant. She closed her eyes in a moment of private prayer and hoped that Lady

Badlesmere would show a greater degree of judgement than her husband had, although she was not hopeful of the outcome.

The next evening, towards sunset they came within sight of Leeds Castle. The king had provided them with a large escort and the queen beckoned forward one of the men-at-arms and instructed him to ride ahead and ask for a night's lodging. Lady de Vescy watched the smile play at Isabella's lips as the man spurred his horse towards the gate house. The queen was enjoying herself, she thought. She had matured into a woman with a cunning mind and a keen interest in politics. With her beside him and Despenser gone, Edward's chances of putting down this rebellion were much increased, she thought.

They walked the horses on, watching to see what would happen, and as the queen had predicted it was not long before the man was seen returning and Lady de Vescy knew what he would have to say.

'My lady,' he announced, 'Lady Badlesmere says that you must seek accommodation elsewhere.'

'Yes!' said the queen and gave Lady de Vescy a smile of satisfaction. 'She has fallen into our trap!' She turned to the sergeant of their guard. 'Take your men,' she commanded him, 'and force an entry. I will not be insulted by this woman's refusal or denied a bed for the night.'

Lady de Vescy was about to ask if that was wise and if it would not be better if they were to ride on to the priory where they would receive a welcome. But she remained silent as she realised that the queen's decision was something she had planned with the king.

They remained at a distance, surrounded by a small guard, as the queen's men approached the castle. A flash of setting sun on metal caught Lady de Vescy's eye and she watched in disbelief as Badlesmere's men took aim from the ramparts and let a volley of arrows fly. A cry of pain echoed across the still air of the late afternoon. A horse shrieked as it was hit and then men began to fall from their saddles.

'This is out of control,' she said to the queen. 'Your guards are being killed. You must recall them, my lady, and we must move on from here. Lady de Vescy was anxious to leave. She was aware that it would take only a small party of determined men to ride out from the castle and take them prisoner. The king's plan would have gone badly wrong if it ended with him having to pay a ransom for the return of his wife. 'We must go!' she told the queen and was relieved when, Isabella, her face filled with panic and fury, reined her horse away from the scene and urged it onto the road to the priory.

★ ★ ★

John de Warenne read the letter twice before the full implications sunk in. Although the king didn't say so it appeared that he had deliberately precipitated the trouble at Leeds Castle and now John was summoned to attend 'with horses and arms and as much power as possible' to 'punish the disobedience and contempt of the queen'. Edward had reason to be angry, conceded John, recalling how he had felt when the Earl of Lancaster had behaved in an insulting manner towards Maud. And it served Badlesmere and his wife right. The man loathed Lancaster yet had for some reason decided to support him. Eble le Strange had done the same thing, but he could see his friend's reason whereas Badlesmere just seemed keen to pick what he thought would be the winning side. But this rebellion was far from over. In fact, it was only just beginning, thought John, as he sent orders for men to be ready in the bailey with their horses and armour, ready to leave at first light on the morrow.

The Earl of Pembroke was already at Leeds

Castle and was in the process of directing his men to begin the siege when John arrived. As his men made camp, John walked around the perimeter with Pembroke. He could make out men from the garrison on the walls of the castle observing them, but they were out of range of their arrows and there was little they could do but watch. It would be a waiting game, thought John, although he suspected that they might not have to wait long. Leeds Castle would not have been expecting a siege and it was unlikely that they were well prepared.

The next day the king arrived in a long procession with his two half-brothers — the earls of Norfolk and Kent. Edward seemed pleased with himself and declared that he would send for his hunting dogs and enjoy some sport whilst he waited for Lady Badlesmere to surrender. He laughed as he told them that Badlesmere himself was at Oxford begging the Contrariants to come to his assistance to break the siege, but that Lancaster had sent letters to his supporters forbidding them to come to Badlesmere's aid.

'It serves him right for turning his back on me and consorting with my enemies,' he said. 'Why would anyone join the cause of a man who hates him? He will learn the error of his ways soon enough.'

The king seemed confident, thought John, and he wondered whose idea this plot had been. The ploy of dividing and conquering his enemies to defeat them seemed too subtle for Edward and John suspected the cunning of Hugh le Despenser was behind it, despite his supposed exile. Rumour was that the man had never even left the country, but was sheltering in the ports along the Kent coast and making a little extra money with forays into piracy. The siege took on the atmosphere of a tournament as men challenged one another in a hastily constructed list as they waited. John scored some pleasing victories and even though the king did not take part he enjoyed watching the sport whilst he was not out with his dogs in the forest.

In the end John was sorry that the castle capitulated so quickly. A mere five days after Edward arrived, a man came out under a flag of truce and handed over the keys. The holiday atmosphere chilled to a serious mood as the king ordered those who had fired arrows at the queen's guard to be brought out. Thirteen men were charged and the king ordered them to be immediately drawn and hanged. John began to protest, but a warning look from Pembroke silenced him. The king had determined to send a message to those who continued to defy him that they now risked death. At least Lady Badlesmere and her children were spared. They were taken to Dover Castle and imprisoned and Edward assured the earls that he would defeat the Contrariants and rid himself of his cousin Lancaster.

★　★　★

Eble le Strange reined in the grey and stared towards the snowy summits of the hills beyond Boroughbridge. Part of the rebel force, led by Roger Mortimer, had been forced to surrender to the king at Shrewsbury and they were fleeing north as an army led by John de Warenne pursued them. Their aim had been to reach Dunstanburgh Castle in Northumberland, in the hope that the Scots would come to their aid, but that seemed impossible now.

If Lancaster had agreed to leave Pontefract sooner they might have stood a chance, thought Eble. But by the time he had been persuaded by Lord Clifford, at the point of a sharp blade, too much time had been lost. The bridge in front of them was being held by Sir Andrew Harcla, and, trapped between two armies, they had little alternative but to stand and fight.

Lancaster had suggested that Harcla might

be open to a bribe. It was so typical of him, thought Eble, that he believed anything could be bought and that any man's morals would melt away at the sight of a few gold coins in a purse. Eble knew that Harcla would not let them across.

Meanwhile the twilight was creeping over the hills. There would be no battle until morning and there was the prospect of an unnerving night ahead of them as they must try to snatch what sleep they could under the threat of enemy spies and surprise attacks.

Before long word came that they were to withdraw to the village and wait for daylight. The plan was to split the army into two columns and whilst those on foot would try to cross the narrow bridge at first light under the command of the Earl of Hereford, the men on horseback were to move downstream and cross at the ford with Lancaster.

Eble followed the dispirited rebel army. Around him he could hear men muttering their discontent and he saw more than a few glance over their shoulders and disappear into the night. If it had not been for his nephews he would probably have followed them. Lancaster was not worth dying for and the chances of crossing the river were low. Their only hope was the arrival of the Scots, but it was a faint hope.

He found a patch of ground, sheltered by the wall of a barn and after tethering the horses he and his nephews wrapped themselves in their cloaks and ate some of the rations they carried with them. It was not worth pitching the tent in case they had to move quickly. They dozed a little, cold and ever on the alert and as the slow dawn came they prepared for battle.

Eble tightened the girth of his saddle and checked that the few personal belongings he might need were secure. Everything else had been packed up and handed to the men in charge of the wagons. He doubted he would see those things again. Even if they were lucky enough to cross the river, the wagons would not escape the king's army. Still, he had got into the habit of travelling light.

'Stay within sight of me,' he told his nephews. 'And don't try to be a bloody hero — either of you!'

'Mihi Parta Tueri! I will fight for what is mine!' said John, repeating their family motto. He briefly clasped gloved hands with Eble and Roger and then turned to his horse. Determination hardened his expression in the moment before his helm concealed his face and Eble muttered a prayer and crossed himself as Lancaster gave the signal that they should move towards the fast flowing river.

Glancing upstream Eble saw the Earl of Hereford leading foot soldiers towards the bridge, but the column disappeared from sight as he followed the other horsemen downstream, around the bend that led to the ford. He could see his breath on the cold morning air as he hung back, wanting to see his nephews cross safely before he urged the grey forwards. But as the first horsemen entered the water there was a shriek of arrows that, for a moment, clouded the sky before falling with deadly accuracy. Eble peered through the slit in his helm as he watched the arrow storm pierce men and horses indiscriminately. Some riders fell, wounded or dead, into the gushing river. Others tried to fling themselves clear as their mounts crumpled beneath them, only to be tugged down into the water by the weight of their armour. The river began to pinken in swirls and eddies as the blood from those being massacred upstream flowed down and mingled with the carnage he was witnessing before him.

The grey tossed its head and whinnied in distress, replying to the screams of the dying horses and men in the river. Eble ducked as another torrent of arrows flew, even though he knew he was beyond their range. He looked around for his nephews, but men and horses all looked the same as they milled in terror at the onslaught. This was madness, he thought. Every last man of them would be killed if someone didn't do something. Then, above the noise, he thought he heard the sound of a horn and when he pulled the horse around he saw that there was a retreat. With a prayer that his nephews would have enough sense to follow him he urged the horse up the bank and back towards Boroughbridge, though he had no intention of remaining there. The only thing he could do now was to find John and Roger and take them back to Knockin where they could at least try to hold the castle.

He didn't dare remove his helm although it severely restricted his vision. And even though it also dulled his hearing it didn't completely block out the screams and moans of the dying. Eble could smell the blood, and the excrement, and he was finding it hard to calm his horse which was tossing its head and snorting with its nostrils flared in panic.

At a distance from the river he slowed his pace and looked back. He felt a wave of relief as he recognised John following him.

'I'm thankful you ride such a distinctive horse,' shouted John when he caught up.

'Where is Roger?'

'He was behind me a moment ago.'

257

Eble narrowed his eyes and saw his other nephew riding towards them. He thanked God that they were safe so far, even if the danger was far from over. He waved the younger men towards the shelter of a small copse of trees and risked pulling off his helm so that they could discuss what to do next.

'It would be more than foolish to stay here,' he told them. 'We do not stand a chance and it will only be a matter of time before Lancaster is taken. I suggest we quietly head back to the borders and lay low until this is resolved.'

'And take the cowards way out?' demanded John. Eble saw indignation flair in his eyes. 'I have pledged my support to the Earl of Lancaster. And I will honour that pledge!' he told him.

'I admire your courage, and your loyalty,' said Eble. 'But if you value your life you will listen to me.'

'Mihi Parta Tueri!' he shouted at him above the sound of the galloping hooves that passed by as other men tried to save themselves. 'I will fight for what is mine! I will not run like some defeated dog!'

'John!' Eble called after him as the boy spurred his horse onto the track that led to Boroughbridge. 'Fool! Damn fool!' he muttered as he watched him go.

'What now?' asked Roger. 'Should we go after him?'

Eble hesitated, but then decided that the risk was too great. He had done as much as he was prepared to do to help John and in any case pursuing him would not make him change his mind.

'Did you bring a cloak and hood in your saddle bag as I told you?' he asked. Roger nodded. 'Then put them on over your armour and let us get as far away from here as possible.'

★　★　★

My tears filled my palms to overflowing. My husband's army had been defeated. Many had been killed and I feared that Eble le Strange was dead.

I could not dismiss from my mind the image of him standing before me and the hurt in his eyes as I had told him angrily to go. I wept now because I had been so stubborn, because I had remained on the window seat and clenched my fists in anger as he had gone from my chamber and closed the door behind him. I had wanted to leap up and run down the steps after him. I had wanted to call him back and give him some small token that would have helped to keep him safe — a ring, a brooch, a lock of my hair, a kiss that would have lingered on his lips and reminded him to have a care for himself and to come back to me. But I had been so angry with him that I had wanted him to go feeling guilty, knowing that he went without my blessing and in defiance of my wishes.

And neither could I dismiss from my memory the feel of his hands as he had grasped my arms. For a moment I had thought that he might push me down onto my back along the window seat and pull up my skirts. It is what my husband would have done. And what had surprised me most was that I would not have objected. Much of my anger had been an attempt to cover the confusion of my feelings. I had challenged him, goaded him, but he had let me go and I was glad and sorry at the same time; although now I was only sorry, because I was sure that he was dead.

I was barely aware of Edith's arm around my shoulders. 'You cannot be sure. Some escaped,' she said, although I knew that her words were just the empty sound of comfort.

'Why did he go?' I asked her. 'I begged him not to abandon me and he would not listen!'

'I'm sure he did what he thought was for the best.'

'No!' I squirmed away from her touch and began to pace the room. 'How could it have been for the best — to go and fight for a man who hated him? It would not surprise me to learn that my husband had killed him, or at least made sure that he was killed. He would do it to spite me. He takes away everything that I love!'

'They say that the Earl of Lancaster was taken prisoner,' said Edith, 'and that the king holds his cousin in the castle at York.'

'I am glad!' I spat. 'I care nothing for him. I hope they have thrown him into the deepest, darkest, rat-infested dungeon that there is!'

'Perhaps you should have a care, my lady,' warned Edith.

'For what?' I asked her.

'For your own safety,' she said with a worried frown. 'If your husband is a traitor, then you are a traitor's wife.'

'But John de Warenne will not allow anyone to harm me. He will ensure that I am safe. Won't he?' I asked as doubt began to gnaw at the corners of my mind.

I sat down again and gave more thought to my husband's plight. After such a rebellion the king would surely not allow him to live. At first the thought pleased me. I hated him so much that it would have given me pleasure to stand and watch as they made him lay his head upon the block. But Edith's words forced me to reconsider my situation. John de Warenne had led the king's army against my husband. I was under his control and was the wife of the man he had taken captive and whom the king meant to charge with treason. I thought back to the way that the king's father had treated the wives of his enemies in Scotland and a prickle of fear ran through me. I did not want to be imprisoned in a cage or forced to take the veil. And if the king and Hugh le Despenser decided that I was to be made an example of, would John de Warenne be able to protect me?

I looked up at Edith and saw the fear on her face.

'Do you think we should leave here?' I asked her. 'Go to where it may not be so easy for the king to find me?'

★ ★ ★

Eble knew that there would be men on the road to the south. Perhaps, he thought, it might be better to stay in the forest. As he allowed the grey to pick its way over the scattered logs and branches he thought it must be nearly noon — his stomach was certainly telling him so — and he knew that if they headed towards the sun they should not go far wrong. He led the way as quietly as he could through the tangle of trees. The woodland concealed them but also made any sight of the enemy more difficult. There were sometimes sounds from a distance — sounds of horses, of men, of voices raised in challenge and Eble became aware that search parties had been sent out by Harcla to capture or kill those who were trying to escape. He pulled his cloak closely around his armour and knew that unless he took off the hauberk and chain leggings he could not hope to pass for an innocent traveller caught in the crossfire of battle. But if it came to a fight the armour would afford some protection and he decided that he would feel too vulnerable without it.

When the moment came, they appeared from nowhere. It was as if the gnarled tree trunks had suddenly been given life and, before he and Roger could draw weapons, there were men all around them. Eble stared at the tips of the arrows, quivering on the bows of the archers. It would take only the flick of a wrist for one to fly, and at this close distance the tips would pierce through his armour and into his flesh, probably deep enough to kill.

'Get down from the horses!' shouted a

voice. 'Throw your weapons to the ground!'

Realising there was no alternative, Eble nodded at Roger to do as they were bid. Under the watchful eyes of Harcla's men he withdrew both sword and knife and threw them down onto the leaf mulch. They were efficiently retrieved and the horses led away. The grey looked back at him as a man grasped its reins and Eble was sorry to see it go. John de Warenne had paid good money for it and he felt that he had let his friend down by allowing it to be forfeit.

A man bound his hands tightly in front of him. The rope cut into his skin. Then the end was tied to the saddle of a horse and a knife was pushed towards his throat.

'I hope you can keep up,' grinned the man, his brown teeth and bad breath wafting a stench into Eble's face.

'Don't worry. It isn't over yet,' said Eble to Roger as he saw the shock etched across his nephew's face. 'All will be well.'

But his words held no comfort for himself. He knew that this rebellion had infuriated the king and although there were those who whispered that Edward was not his father's son, his temper and his need for revenge belied that claim. Eble knew that many would die.

Hours later they were just two more

prisoners in a line of tightly tethered men who were forced to march behind the horses. It was not easy to keep up the constant pace, but he gritted his teeth and made no protest. It would have been futile anyway. Roger was behind him and Eble, unable to look around, prayed that he was coping. He guessed that they were being taken to York, but even at this pace night would have fallen before they arrived.

★   ★   ★

Eble was pushed into a wet and freezing cold dungeon. As he sank down, exhausted, he felt the water seep through the thin linen of his braies. His cloak and armour had been stripped from him and after a moment he began to shiver violently. Men were collapsing around him with groans in the blackness and he reached out his still tethered hands to touch one or two and whisper 'Roger?' But he could not find his nephew and Eble prayed that he had survived the long and unrelenting journey.

He recoiled as he felt something warm on his bare foot. Even without seeing it he knew it was a rat and not another human that had touched him. He found the wall and though it was dripping wet he leant his aching back against it, pulled his knees up to his chest and closed his eyes — though whether his eyes were closed or open made no difference now that the faint light from the torches had been obliterated by the thudding shut of the door.

Eble prayed. Not words of his own, but the words of the familiar prayers — the Pater Noster, the Ave Maria. The words calmed him a little and soothed his mind. He must have fallen momentarily asleep, but the fall of his head jerked him awake again. He did not dare lie down on the wet straw for fear of being bitten to death by the rats, so he laid his forehead on his knees. Maybe he slept again. He didn't know. It was as if he existed in a place removed from time, like those condemned to live for an eternity in purgatory.

★   ★   ★

John de Warenne led a party of armed men into the courtyard of the castle at York. The sun was shining in a fresh blue sky, but it was the prospect of being revenged on Thomas of Lancaster that lifted his spirits more than the promise of springtime.

When the king had asked him to bring the prisoner from York to the castle at Pontefract there had been no doubt in John's mind about his purpose. Edward wanted revenge for the murder of Piers Gaveston and Lancaster's days were numbered.

'Show me the prisoner,' he said, anticipating the sight of his enemy being held in a dungeon. He hoped that they had put him in the worst place they could find and not afforded him any luxury. But even so, he was shocked when the trapdoor was lifted and he saw Lancaster cowering in the corner of the festering cell, blinking and trying to shade his eyes from the piercing shaft of sunlight that fell onto him. He had been stripped of all his clothing but his underlinen which he had soiled and the smell that rose was abhorrent.

'Pull him out and wash him down,' said John. 'I don't want to smell that all the way back to Pontefract.' And he watched as the man was dragged up into the daylight and buckets of icy water were thrown over him, leaving him to stand shivering and steaming.

Lancaster looked up and after wiping his eyes recognised him. 'You will pay for this!' he exploded.

There were years of hurt and frustration in the blow that John struck, though he had to quell an unexpected moment of pity as Lancaster reeled, bleeding, to his knees and wiped at his nose with his hands. Was it cowardly to strike a bound and unarmed

267

man, John wondered, but he dismissed the thought. He had not vowed for so many years to make Thomas of Lancaster sorry to be beset by compassion now.

'Secure him to a horse and bring out the other prisoners,' he told the guards.

John watched as the men were hauled into the open. They had been taken with Lancaster as they hid in a small chapel at Boroughbridge and the king had ordered their executions also. They had been stripped of their clothes and their identities and John de Warenne walked down the line, demanding each man's name before he was fastened to the cart.

'John le Strange, lord of Knockin,' said the last one. John stared at him for so long that the boy raised his eyes. There was no doubt of his identity. His resemblance to Eble was unmistakeable. This was the nephew that his friend had vowed to help. It seemed that the gesture had been futile and John wondered if Eble too had been taken prisoner.

'Take him,' he said and watched as the boy went, unprotesting, to join the other marcher lords. He wished that he could help him, but his ready admission to his identity had already condemned him. He was a traitor and would be executed.

'Where are the other prisoners?' he asked.

'I would like to be certain that there are no more Contrariants amongst them.'

The guard looked doubtful, but John insisted and was led down the steep stairway to the dungeon. The stench was nauseating and John fought the urge to vomit as the door was unlocked and opened. He gestured to a guard to go inside ahead of him with a torch and to light the faces of the prisoners one by one. None looked familiar and he was beginning to believe that Eble had escaped when the smoky flame illuminated a head of fair hair, the face averted.

'Bring that man to me,' he said. Eble looked up with an expression of confusion and hope as he recognised his voice but had the good sense to say nothing. 'He is a member of my household and has been taken in error,' he said. 'Find him some clean clothes and then send him to me.'

'My lord,' said Eble as he was pulled to his feet. John gave him a warning look, afraid that he would give himself away. 'There is another member of your household here. A man by the name of Roger.'

For a moment John wondered if Eble were so badly hurt that he was babbling, but he nodded to the guards who called out for anyone named Roger. After a few minutes one was brought out for his inspection whose resemblance to both Eble and John le Strange confirmed all John needed to know. 'Yes,' he lied. 'He is also of my household.'

★   ★   ★

Edith and I packed what valuables we could carry, stitched coins and jewels into the hems of our garments and, having made it known that we would take a short ride, we left the castle. Once out of sight, we gathered our skirts, sat astride our horses and rode fast towards Lincolnshire. There was a small manor at Swaveton which had once belonged to my mother's family and was part of my dower lands where I knew I would be offered a welcome.

There was much unrest in the country as we headed north, trying not to draw attention to ourselves. The roads were muddied and rutted, filled with ice-covered puddles where the armies of men and horses and carts had passed by. At the inns where we stayed there was an atmosphere of suspicion. Whether someone recognised me or whether it was pure chance I would never know, but as we were heading up the great north road we came upon a party of armed men who seemed to have been lying in wait. As soon as I saw the king's colours under their heavy cloaks my hope of reaching Swaveton began to dissipate along with the early morning mist.

The horses blocked the road and as I glanced back I saw more men, materialising from the foggy undergrowth and preventing us turning back south. I reined in the little mare and wondered if I could affect a fall from the saddle and try to run. There were trees not too far distant and I might be able to slip in amongst them and evade the pursuit. The hunter did not always catch the prey.

'My lady,' the man greeted me.

I inclined my head slightly, allowing the hood to fall further over my face and wishing that Eble were seated behind me, his strong and reassuring arm clasped around my waist. But I was alone now and could rely only on my own wits to escape.

'Where are you headed?' asked the man.

'Into Lincolnshire,' I replied as my mare backed away from his skittish stallion.

'To where exactly?'

'What business is it of yours?' I asked.

'My business is to search the countryside for traitors, my lady, and convey them to the king.'

'Then you have no business with me, and I would be grateful if you would allow us to pass by,' I replied, striving to keep my tone steady even though my heart raced and my fingers trembled on the reins, conveying my fear to the mare.

'I admire your courage, my lady,' said the man. 'But you do not deceive me. I know your face even though you strive to keep it hidden.'

'What nonsense you speak,' I replied. 'I think you should go about your search for traitors instead of delaying me here.'

'Do you deny that you are the wife of the traitor, Lancaster?' he asked. 'And before you answer, my lady, pause and consider that I know you well even though my face may be just one amongst many to you.'

I looked at him again. It was possible that he knew me.

'You mistake me for another,' I told him. 'I am no traitor to the king.'

'Even so, my lady, it may be wise to allow me to escort you on your journey.'

'You would escort me to my manor in Lincolnshire? That is a generous offer. But I will not delay you from your urgent duties on behalf of the king.'

'Do not toy with me, my lady,' said the man. 'I know who you are and I also know that the king will reward me well for taking you to York. Will you allow me to escort you?

Or shall I have my men seize you by force?'

I hesitated and at his signal an armed man rode forward and took the reins of my horse. Another grasped the bridle of Edith's mount and began to lead her away as she protested loudly, but hopelessly.

'My lady, I must insist that you come with me,' said the man.

24

Eble watched as Thomas of Lancaster was tied to a horse for the journey to Pontefract. There had been talk of making him walk, barefoot, but in the end John had judged it better, and quicker, to at least put the man facing backwards upon a nag — although he had not considered it necessary to offer him any clothing and, with a borrowed cloak to keep him warm, Eble tried not to pity Lancaster as he shivered in the bitter wind clad only in his wet linen. If the king did not kill him then surely a chill would invade his lungs and do the deed instead.

There was still deep snow on the northern roads as they left the castle at York to ride to Pontefract. The crowds that watched them leave, made balls of it with their hands and flung them at Lancaster, jeering at him and shouting that he would now receive the reward he had for a long time deserved. Many had come from the outlying villages and towns to mock the man they believed had encouraged the Scots to burn and ravage their homes and crops in his attempts to win the crown of England for himself.

One snowball narrowly missed Eble as a small boy took anyone in the procession for a legitimate target and as he glared at the child its mother put a protective arm around it. She met Eble's eyes and mouthed a fearful apology. Eble smiled in reassurance. If he had had a coin he would have thrown it to her, but he had not even a purse let alone money and was completely dependent on the goodwill of John de Warenne. If it had not been for his friend both he and Roger would still have been fearing for their lives in the stinking prison.

One of the snowballs hit Lancaster full in the face and almost knocked him from the horse. Peals of laughter rang out and Eble saw John de Warenne smile. Eble recalled the day at Pontefract when they were squires and Lancaster and his friends had pelted them with similar missiles — though balls of hard and cutting ice rather than the soft snow of a playful attack. One had cut John badly on the forehead and under the hair that he always combed to cover it he still bore the scar. It had been just one of the many occasions on which John had vowed that he would make Lancaster regret what he had done. And now that day had come.

Lancaster's linen was frozen to him by the time they reached Pontefract Castle. Eble was not surprised to see Hugh le Despenser back at the king's side and when Lancaster was dragged from his horse, Despenser began to shout vile insults into his face.

'And now the tower that you built to imprison the king will be your dungeon — for the rest of your life! Though do not count on that being for long!' he raged as he poked a finger into Lancaster's ribs at every word. 'You will die, you bastard scum! Just as you deserve to!'

Then guards dragged Lancaster away, across the frozen ground which he had once been able to call his own, to the secure tower that he had ordered built and he was thrown inside as Despenser returned to the king. Eble watched as Edward put an arm around Hugh's shoulders and they went into Lancaster's hall to warm themselves at his hearth and eat his food and drink his wine.

★   ★   ★

John de Warenne took his place at the table in the hall of Pontefract Castle. He had slept badly and in the hours that he had lain awake he had questioned why it should be so. For how many years had he waited to be revenged on Thomas of Lancaster? He had expected that to see his enemy brought so low on the wheel of fortune would have given him such pleasure as to afford him a deep and undreaming sleep, but the fate of the man reminded him that all those who rose to power could be brought low and the lesson had unsettled him.

The other earls who were to sit in judgement joined him at table — Pembroke, the king's half-brother Kent, Hugh le Despenser and his father, the justice Robert Malberthorpe and finally the king himself, his fur lined gown magnificent against the cold and in contrast to the filthy prisoner who was dragged before them.

The charges consisted of a list of the long held grievances of Edward towards his cousin. Every wrong was itemised and even included the way that Lancaster had shouted insults at him as he had passed by Pontefract Castle five years ago. Nothing had been forgotten, no insult, real or imagined, had been overlooked — although John and everyone in the hall knew that it was for the execution of Piers Gaveston that the king most desired his revenge.

The evidence was conclusive but as he was grasped by the arms to be taken away Lancaster showed one last flourish of anger.

'This is a powerful court, and great in authority, where no answer is heard nor any excuse admitted!' he shouted. But his words, in the hall where he had once ruled, in the castle where his bullying had never ceased, were meaningless. The sentence was hanging, drawing and quartering, which the king, in his regard for Lancaster's status, had commuted to beheading. And in a parody of Piers Gaveston's death they took Lancaster to a hill outside the walls — the one where he had stood and jeered and hooted at the king. And facing Scotland, to remind him that no help had come from those hills, he was made to kneel and his head was struck from his body with three blows of the axe.

★ ★ ★

We passed a night at Pontefract Castle on our way to York. I asked that I might sleep one last time in the chamber that had been familiar to me as a child and as Edith helped to make me ready for my bed I walked to the window and looked down.

'That is where my brother John fell from the turret and was killed,' I told her, pointing to the spot. 'If he had lived, or if my elder brother Edmund had not drowned at Denbigh, I would never have been brought to this. My lady mother would sit beside this hearth and tell stories,' I said as I returned to the bench and allowed Edith to comb my hair. 'My favourite was that of the Lady Melette of the White Tower. Do you know it?'

'Indeed I do, my lady,' said Edith.

'I hoped for a husband like Guarin de Metz. I wanted a man who was brave and handsome and who would care for me and protect me. Instead I got Thomas of Lancaster.'

'He was no Guarin de Metz,' agreed Edith. 'But do not forget the man who rescued you from your husband.'

'Eble le Strange,' I said as I picked up a loose hair that had fallen onto my gown and began to twist it around my fingers. 'When he came for me at Canford I thought that he was my Guarin. But Guarin would never have abandoned the Lady Melette to her fate. He would never have allowed her to be brought so low. I am afraid, Edith,' I told her as I brushed the hair to the floor. 'I am afraid of how the king will punish me even though I have committed no sin against him, except to be the wife of his enemy.'

'I am sure he will show you compassion, my lady.'

'I am not so sure,' I said. 'His temper is a terrible thing and now that Despenser is returned from exile he will listen to his advice again — and he is by all accounts a vicious and a greedy man.'

★ ★ ★

'I am sorry, Eble,' said John. 'I made a plea for his life, but Despenser has the king's ear again, and he would not countenance any pardon for your nephew. He was executed this morning.'

Eble crossed himself before dropping his face into his palms. He wished that he could weep, but he was so tired that even tears eluded him. He wanted to thank his friend for his attempt to save the life of the boy, but his fuddled mind refused to form any coherent words.

'You cannot help the dead,' said John, 'except to go and light a candle and say prayers for his soul. And when that is done you need to turn your attention to the living. I think you may also be in danger.'

Eble looked up through spread fingers. His eyes ached and a drum rhythm was beating the inside of his temples. His nose would not stop running and every so often a fit of sneezing overcame him. He felt hopeless. The nephew he had tried to help was dead, he hoped without too much pain, and although he had saved Roger and himself the news that their lives might still be in danger was almost too much for him to deal with. All he wanted to do was creep to his pallet and sleep.

'When the king signed the death warrant for your nephew he asked if you were the heir,' went on John, 'and I had to tell him that the new lord of Knockin was your younger nephew Roger. He asked about him; wanted to know if he had fought with his brother. And he asked about your loyalty. I lied, of course, but Despenser was there, as always, listening with that inscrutable expression on his face.'

Eble groaned and sniffed. 'So you think the king will confiscate the land anyway?' he asked. 'If so I would have been better off staying with Alicia. It has all been for nothing, and she hates me for it. And what of her?' he asked. 'I hope that you have kept her safe through all this.'

He looked up when John did not reassure him straight away. 'Where is Alicia? Is she safe?'

'She has left Reigate. I do not know where she is.'

Eble got to his feet, fists clenched.

'She was never my prisoner!' protested John, standing his ground. They glared at one another for a moment. Then Eble's nose began to itch and he sneezed again and again, rendering him momentarily helpless. 'I only know because the king has demanded that she is brought to York. I sent an escort but they returned to tell me that she went out to ride with her maid and never returned.'

'If any harm has come to her I will hold you responsible!' threatened Eble, wiping his nose on the back of his hand.

'If you cared so much about her then why did you leave her to fight alongside her husband?' shouted John.

Eble reeled at the words. What John had said hurt him more than any blow could have done.

'Eble, you must take Roger and go back to the marches,' said John. 'Neither of you is safe here. Put some distance between yourselves and the king. I may be able to reason with him, given time, convince him that you were with me and that you and Roger are loyal.'

'We will go tomorrow,' said Eble, sitting down again. He was weary and could not bear the thought of the cold journey.

'Go now,' said John. 'Find your nephew, take two of my horses and go. And do not think to go seeking Alicia,' he warned. 'She will be discovered soon enough and brought here. And I promise that I will do everything I can to protect her.'

'If anyone should protect her it ought to be me,' said Eble.

'And do you think the king will listen to

you?' demanded John. 'See sense, Eble! If you stay here there is nothing you can do for Alicia. You will only get yourself killed. Go back to Knockin. I still have some influence over the king, despite Despenser. I will not let him harm her. She was under my protection. The king cannot think that she was in any way involved in this rebellion.' Eble felt his friend's arm warm and comforting around his shoulders. 'Have we not always looked out for one another?' asked John. 'I know that you are tired and ill, but you must go.'

25

There was a slow thaw as we approached York, although the snow still clung to the tops of the hills. When I saw the tower of the minster I felt glad that the journey was almost ended, but I was fearful that I might be locked in a dungeon — or worse.

We rode past the huts of the people who lived outside the city walls, skirted St Mary's abbey and then went under the arch of the Bootham Bar where the portcullis was raised and the guards waved us through. We pushed along the crowded streets and the sight of the meat on the butcher's shelves along the Shambles made me imagine the quartering of those who had died a traitor's death. At least my husband, much as I had hated him, had been spared that indignity and his body had been buried by the monks in the priory church at Pontefract.

I glanced at Edith as we approached the castle ramparts. She was staring at all the armed men who wore the king's colours. The city and the castle were under close guard and even the curious citizens who had followed our progress seemed subdued.

The gate was opened for us and we were escorted inside. I watched as it was closed again. I was trapped. There was no escape for me and I was entirely reliant on the king's mercy.

I waved away the man who came towards me and dismounted without help.

'So you are the Countess of Lancaster,' he said as he looked me up and down. 'You are not what I expected.'

I stared back at him, expecting him to bow or make some show of manners, but his eyes were steady and self-important.

'And neither is my welcome!' I snapped back. 'I am accustomed to being shown some respect!'

'Since when have the wives of traitors been worthy of respect?' he asked.

'My only sin is to have been married to a man I hated and despised,' I told him. 'And lately I have been under the protection of the Earl of Surrey, whose loyalty is in no doubt. Who are you anyway?' I asked.

'My name is Sir Hugh le Despenser,' he said. 'I am the king's chamberlain.'

'Then I expect you to bow before you speak to me,' I told him. There was something about the haughty look in his blue eyes that made me afraid but I was determined not to show my fear. He was below me in rank, recently exiled and by all accounts had made his living as a pirate like a common criminal. Looking at him I could believe that he was entirely ruthless, though his false smile demonstrated that he could also make use of his charm.

'Let us not begin with a misunderstanding,' he said. 'I see that you are cold and tired so I will forgive your outburst.' He nodded to a group of men who were standing at a respectful distance. 'Take the lady and her maid to the chamber that has been prepared,' he said before turning back to me. 'I will come to see you on the morrow when you have rested,' he said, 'and we can discuss what your future holds.'

I was about to tell him that I would speak with no one but the king himself, but my elbow was firmly grasped and I was propelled across the courtyard, through a doorway and up some steep steps.

There was now no doubt in my mind that I was a prisoner although I was thankful to see that the chamber had a hearth in which logs were blazing. There was a bed with mattresses that looked thick and clean and Edith was allowed to remain with me. Food was brought in and good wine and even hot water, and Edith helped me to strip off my wet clothes and wash myself. When I was finished she wrapped a cover from the bed tightly around me and handed me a cup of wine.

'What will become of us?' she asked at last.

'I don't know.' I shook my head and sipped at the wine. 'At least we are treated well, for now.'

I slept fitfully, waking again and again to the sounds of voices, footsteps and moaning. At dawn I pushed back the covers and prayed on my knees beside the bed. Edith joined me and we recited the Pater Noster aloud in whispered voices. My clothes were dirty from the long journey but I allowed Edith to dress me in them and braid my hair and pin it around my head.

We were provided with more bread and some cheese. The stubs of the candles in the sconces were replaced by new ones and Edith fastened back the skin that covered the small window so that a trickle of sunlight fell across the floor. But I would not go to look outside. I was afraid that I would catch sight of men hanging from the gibbets. The air in the courtyard stank of death.

Around mid-morning Hugh le Despenser came into the chamber. I saw Edith freeze as she stared at him. He snapped his fingers at her.

'Leave us!' he commanded.

'But . . . '

'Leave!' he repeated without looking at her again. His eyes were fixed on me, although I did not look at him but watched as Edith hesitated and then went from the room. The door shut behind her and I was left alone with Despenser.

He came to sit beside me on the bench, his knee almost touching mine. He reached out his hands to the blaze, held them there for a moment and then rubbed them together.

'It is still cold,' he said. 'But I think the last of the snow will be gone by the end of the week.'

'I had not expected you to come to me to make idle talk,' I said, sounding more confident than I felt.

He raised an eyebrow and a smile pulled at the corners of his lips. 'What did you expect, my lady?' he asked.

'I do not know,' I replied. 'I do not know why the king has summoned me here.'

'Really?' He watched me and I thought of Tabby and the way that he would play with a mouse, how he would trick it into thinking that it was safe, even give it its freedom for a moment, before finally bringing his paw down on its head. But every so often he would miscalculate and the mouse would scuttle away. Sometimes it would run into a hole and become trapped as Tabby sniffed and yowled at the entrance. Other mice were quicker and luckier. They escaped altogether. I wondered what manner of mouse I would turn out to be.

'I know nothing that I have done to displease the king,' I told Despenser. 'Why am I kept here and denied my liberty?'

'You are not what I expected,' he said again as he watched me carefully. 'I thought that you would be fearful and cowed, that marriage to Lancaster would have taught you to be obedient and subservient. Yet, I see that you have spirit. I like that in a woman.'

I think he heard my sharp intake of breath as I began to fear why he had sent Edith away. They said that he was the king's lover but he had a wife too and had fathered children. And I already knew from my husband that some men used the physical act of procreation as a weapon to prove their domination.

'You have no need to fear me,' he smiled. He looked me up and down again. 'Your gown is soiled,' he remarked. 'I will make enquiries into clothing and your maid may choose something appropriate.'

With a nod of the head he stood up, called to the guard to let him out and I was left alone and unsure of the purpose of his visit.

When there was a sharp rap at my door early the next morning I expected it to be Despenser again and I got up from the bench and stood as tall as I could to face him, brushing stray crumbs from the skirts of the clean gown. When I saw that it was John de Warenne I was torn between relief and anger. The expression in his steady grey eyes was unfathomable. He gave a slight bow but I kept my hands clasped together so that he could not take one to kiss it, and for a moment my gaze strayed to a place behind him. But he was alone and I chided myself for the foolish hope that Eble le Strange might be with him.

'My lady,' said John. He turned to ensure that the door was closed then took my arm to draw me away from it. 'Why did you leave Reigate?' he asked quietly, although his eyes flashed with annoyance.

I glanced towards Edith who had busied herself with the bed covers. 'I thought I would be safer in Lincolnshire,' I said. 'Whilst I was at Reigate the king knew where to find me.'

'You could not have avoided him wherever you went, unless you planned to take ship abroad,' said John. 'At least whilst you were under my protection I had some control over the matter. But to run only serves to make you look guilty.'

'Guilty? But you know that I had no part in this rebellion.'

'Which is why I was so damned angry when I heard that you had left Reigate! I am doing my best to protect you, Alicia, but you are not helping yourself!'

I was about to reprimand him and tell him that he had no right to speak to me in that manner, but his anger frightened me because I saw that it was a sign of his desperation.

'What will happen to me?' I asked.

'If it were just the king I could persuade him to be benevolent towards you, but Despenser has his ear and God alone knows what he is planning, but whatever it is it will be for his benefit and not yours. All the lands that Lancaster had from his father are forfeit to the king and probably a good many of the ones that were your father's. My best advice is to be meek and co-operative and I will do my best to ensure that you leave here alive.'

'Alive?' A shiver ran through me. 'You do not think that . . . ?'

'I do not know what to think,' he replied. 'The whole country is in disarray. Many are dead already and there will be more deaths to come.'

'Eble?' His name sounded strange on my tongue and I prepared myself to hear bad news.

'He is alive,' John reassured me.

'Where is he now?

'I sent him back to Knockin. Do not blame him, Alicia,' said John. 'We have all had to make hard choices and it does not mean that he loves you less.'

I nodded. I knew that John spoke the truth and I regretted the manner in which I had sent Eble away. It would have torn my soul apart to hear that he had gone to his death believing that I was still angry with him. I felt John's hand close over mine. 'He wanted to wait here when he heard that the king had sent for you,' he said. 'I had the devil of a job persuading him to go, but he is safer in the marches until I can ask Edward to grant him a pardon and letters of safe conduct.'

★   ★   ★

John watched as Hugh le Despenser reached for the jug and filled the king's cup himself, waving away the page whose task it was. Edward smiled at the man affectionately. It made John's flesh crawl.

'We cannot allow Alicia de Lacy to retain her lands or her titles,' Despenser told him in response to the appeal he had made on Alicia's behalf.

'But the countess is loyal,' argued John. 'She had already left her husband and put herself under my protection.' He was irritated that the king had not invited him to sit down and that he was forced to stand in the presence of this man who was showing signs of becoming a far more dangerous influence on Edward than Gaveston had ever been.

'This man, Eble le Strange, who you sent to fetch her from Canford,' said Despenser. 'How well do you know him?'

'Very well. We were squires together at Pontefract under the care of the late Earl of Lincoln.'

'But how well do you really know him?' continued Despenser. 'Was he not a member of Lancaster's household?'

'That is true,' agreed John.

'And you must have heard the rumours?'

'I hear a lot of rumours,' replied John impatiently. 'Most of them are untrue.'

'How did le Strange come to be in your service rather than Lancaster's?' asked Despenser.

'What is this? A court of law?' demanded John angrily. 'Sire,' he said, appealing to the king. 'Am I to be questioned as if there is doubt about my loyalty?'

'Answer the question, John,' said the king. 'Hugh is very astute in these matters and I think that what he has suggested may be correct.'

'What has he suggested?' asked John, looking back at Despenser.

'There is common talk that Alicia de Lacy and this le Strange are lovers,' said Despenser.

'Eble le Strange has known the countess since childhood. He was her squire and the head of her household at Pickering.'

'And her lover?'

'I do not know,' said John.

'Oh come,' laughed Despenser. 'First you tell me that you and Eble le Strange have been friends since childhood and that you know him well, then you claim that you do not know if he is her lover. I find that hard to believe.'

'Believe what you will!' snapped John. 'What business is it of yours anyway?'

'It is my business because I am here to advise the king!' shouted Despenser, getting to his feet and planting his palms firmly on the trestle. 'You may deny the truth — for whatever reason — maybe you think to defend this man you claim is your friend, but common talk says that he is Alicia de Lacy's lover!' John felt for his sword. But the sheath was empty, the weapon having been surrendered at the door. He glared at Despenser who sat down and leaned back in the chair, satisfied that he had riled him. John fought the urge to leap over the table and grab him by the throat.

'Why did le Strange leave the service of the Earl of Lancaster?' asked Despenser, pressing the tips of his thumbs and fingers together.

'Lancaster set us against one another in a joust,' said John and briefly explained the circumstances.

'And you took him into your own service?'

'Yes.'

'And it was he who suggested the rescue of Lancaster's wife?'

'No. It was . . . it was a decision made by several of us, with the king's consent.' John glanced at Edward who had leaned forward with his elbows on the trestle.

'But you sent le Strange to fetch her? Why?' asked Despenser.

'She knew him well and had reason to trust him.'

'Because they are lovers,' concluded Despenser with a satisfied slap of his hand upon the table. 'There you have your proof, my lord,' he said to Edward.

John was puzzled. He was still unsure

exactly what it was Despenser was trying to prove to the king.

'Even if that were true. What difference does it make?' he asked. 'The countess hated her husband and was in no way involved with this rebellion.'

'No?' demanded Despenser, getting up again and leaning across the trestle. 'Are you blind as well as stupid?'

'Sire,' appealed John. 'Your chamberlain has no right to address me in this way.'

'Hugh,' said the king, pulling gently on Despenser's sleeve. 'Sit down and tell the Earl of Surrey what you suspect.'

'You say that le Strange was a member of your household?' asked Despenser.

'Yes.'

'So he was amongst the men who fought alongside you?'

'He ... he ... ' John hesitated, not knowing how much Despenser knew.

'I take it that your answer is no,' he replied with a smug smile. 'Le Strange,' he went on in a conversational tone. 'The family are lords of Knockin, are they not?'

'Yes,' replied John, 'but I don't see what it has to do with this discussion.'

'Really?' remarked Despenser, with a raised eyebrow. 'I think the fact that the le Stranges are marcher lords is very pertinent to our discussion — especially when the man's nephew has just been executed for treason — for joining a rebellion against the king! And if Eble le Strange did not fight in your army who did he fight for? Did he fight with his nephew?'

'I do not know,' lied John.

'Do not know. Do not know,' repeated Despenser. 'The man is a member of your household and you do not know for whom he fought? I put it to you that this man is a traitor, and that he left your household to fight alongside his nephew for the Earl of Lancaster!'

'Eble le Strange had every reason to hate Lancaster,' argued John.

'He may not have been loyal to Lancaster, but he is loyal to Lancaster's wife. Perhaps he thinks that the widow will now become his wife and he can style himself earl!' Despenser banged his fist onto the trestle, making the board leap, and glared at John in triumph. 'And that is why Alicia de Lacy cannot be permitted to keep anything!' There was a reverberating silence as the men in the room stared at one another. The silence held, taught as a stretched bow string, until Despenser spoke again. 'Do you know where le Strange is now?' he asked John.

'Sire,' pleaded John. 'I gave the man

permission to go home. His nephew is dead and has a young wife. I thought it best that he should break the news to her. But he is no traitor. I will vouch for his loyalty.'

'Even so,' said Edward. 'I think that Hugh is right when he says that Alicia must be stripped of her lands. Her connection with this marcher lord makes it too risky for her to keep them. We do not want her to be used as the focal point for another rebellion, do we?'

'No sire,' said John as he inclined his head in obeisance to the king's will, then turned a contemptuous look on Despenser. He would benefit from this and his smile betrayed that he knew it.

★　★　★

Hugh le Despenser went ahead of me down the twisting steps from my chamber. One of his men came behind, the edge of his sword catching the stone wall at every step. The entrance to the great hall was guarded by armed men on either side of the door, although it was opened without hesitation as we approached.

Despenser turned and made a slight bow as he indicated that I should precede him to the trestle where a document was laid out for my signature. A mere formality, he had explained, and then I would be free to go back to Lincolnshire unmolested.

The hall was quiet, as if the servants had been denied access, and I looked back as the door was closed behind us and Despenser's man stood in front of it with his arms folded across his broad chest. There were no scribes, just several sharpened quills set beside the ink. Despenser picked one up, dipped the nib into the black ink, wiped it carefully on the edge of the pot and held it out towards me.

'Here,' he said indicating with his forefinger the place where he wanted me to sign my name.

I made no move to take the quill from his hand as I approached the trestle and glanced at the neatly inscribed document.

'My father taught me never to put my name to anything without reading it first,' I told him. Despenser frowned and a drip of ink slid from the quill onto the trestle, soaking a dark circle into the wood.

'If you insist,' he said with a barb of irritation in his voice and he replaced the quill in the pot and took a step back as I turned the parchment towards a shaft of light from a high window.

As I read, it became clear that the document to which Despenser expected me to add my signature and seal was an agreement to pay a huge indemnity of twenty thousand pounds to the king. The payment of such a huge sum of money would mean not only the loss of the lands that had passed from my father to my husband, but the loss of my own dower lands and everything that I had inherited from my mother as well. I heard myself gasp and I clutched at the edge of the board. I felt someone take my elbow and guide me to a stool. There was a snap of fingers and a cup of wine was placed in my hands and guided to my mouth. I coughed as the liquid touched the back of my throat and wondered what had been added to it. My eyes focused and I saw Despenser standing over me. His expression was one of frustration rather than concern as I looked up.

'Do you feel better now, my lady?' he asked.

'Yes,' I said, wondering if I could have misunderstood what I had just read.

'Then perhaps you would be so good as to sign the document now,' he said. He stalked back to the trestle and took up the quill once more, waiting for me to join him. 'Will you read it to me?' I asked without moving from the stool.

'I'm sure, my lady, that you have already read it for yourself. I do not take you for an illiterate.' His tone was filled with contempt and it was only my belief that he would not hesitate to strike me back harder that prevented me from slapping his face for his insolence.

'I read it, but could not believe my eyes,' I replied. 'It seemed to suggest that I should pay the king everything that I have in return for my freedom.'

'Your husband was a traitor. As a traitor's wife you should think yourself fortunate to escape with your life let alone your freedom,' replied Despenser, holding out the quill again.

'But the Lancaster and Leicester estates are already forfeit to the king. To pay this as well means that I will be left with nothing at all.'

'I am sure that the king will allow you to keep a manor or two. We do not wish to leave you destitute. Perhaps somewhere in Lincolnshire? It is, after all, at the furthest side of the country from the Welsh marches and you would be safer there.'

'Safer?' I asked.

'From the rebel marcher lords. I would not like to see you abducted by one of them for a second time.'

'I was not abducted. I willingly put myself into the protection of the Earl of Surrey,' I said. 'I wish to speak with the king.' I knew that if I could speak to Edward myself I could convince him that he had no reason to doubt my loyalty, or that of Eble le Strange.

'The king is otherwise engaged,' said Despenser and dipped the quill into the ink once more. 'Will you sign the document, my lady?'

It was not a question but a command and I rebelled against it.

'No,' I replied, thinking how angry John de Warenne would be when he heard that I had not heeded his advice to be meek and co-operative. 'I will sign nothing until I have spoken to the king.'

Despenser threw the quill down and snapped his fingers again at the man guarding the door. 'Take her back to her chamber!' he said.

'No!' I protested as the man came towards me. I got to my feet and threw the cup of wine into his face as he reached to grasp my arm. In an instant Despenser was at my side and had my wrist enclosed fiercely in his hand. He wrenched me towards the door, almost jerking my shoulder from its socket. I cried out in pain and he paused to look down at me. His mouth was a thin and taught line, and his whole face was dark with suppressed rage although his voice remained calm and reasonable.

'I will speak with you again when you have had time to give the matter some more thought,' he told me and pushed me towards the guard who was wiping his face on his sleeve.

As I was passed from one man to the other and taken back to the upper chamber, my resolve was replaced by a growing fear. When Edith was allowed in with our dinner I told her in urgent whispers what Despenser had asked me to sign.

'Twenty thousand pounds?' repeated Edith with wide eyes. The amount was more than she could comprehend.

'Everything that I have,' I said. 'My father's lands, my mother's lands, everything. I would be reduced to nothing, to nobody.'

I remembered how precious I had felt when I was growing up at Pontefract. Be careful Mistress Alicia, I had been reminded time without number. But now there was only Edith to remind me.

'You must be careful,' she whispered with a worried glance towards the shadow of the guard on the wall beyond the door. 'Despenser may choose an easier way to gain your lands if you refuse to sign.'

I saw from the look on her face that there was something she was keeping from me.

'What have you heard?' I demanded.

She shook her head. 'It is just kitchen gossip — about your husband. There is a rumour of a miracle at his place of execution.'

'A miracle?' I stared at her, wondering if the confinement was causing her to lose her senses. 'What sort of miracle?' I asked, wild images of my husband risen from the dead and coming back to claim me as his wife tormenting my imagination.

Edith began to fidget with the bread and cheese, dividing it into portions so that she wouldn't have to look at me. 'There was a blind priest who dreamed that if he went to where the execution took place he would regain his sight,' she told me as I sat down at the small table and she placed the food in front of me. 'He had the same dream for three nights and so he went to the hill and he prayed to God and to Thomas of Lancaster.'

I could not believe that I was hearing of such blasphemy. There were plenty of times that I had prayed to God and the Holy Virgin to save me from my husband but I could not imagine him as the recipient of anyone's prayers, and could only think that the poor priest must have been sorely disappointed. Why would a man like my husband, who had done no good deed whilst alive, be any better once he was dead?

'The priest laid his hand on the ground

where the earl was killed and a drop of his dried blood stuck to his fingers and when he wiped his eyes his sight was restored.'

'And where is this priest now,' I scoffed. 'Let him come before us and make an oath and repeat his claim. Then I might give it some credence.'

'You may not give it credence, my lady, but there are plenty who do. Pilgrims are already flocking to the tomb at Pontefract to pray, and saying that your husband was a martyr. And there is talk of your being to blame for your husband's death.

'Me?' I asked. 'In what way do they blame me?'

'There is talk that you plotted with the Earl of Surrey to rid yourself of your husband. There is talk that John de Warenne is your lover, even that you have many lovers . . . that there was witchcraft . . . ' She stopped and looked down at her trencher with a flush on her cheeks as I stared at her in horror. 'I'm sorry. But I am only repeating what I have heard, my lady,' she said.

★ ★ ★

Eble stared at the friars who were sitting at the dinner table in Knockin castle, helping themselves to the dishes of food as if they hadn't eaten for a week. He could scarcely believe the tales they were relating.

'And then there was a child who had been drowned in the town well at Pontefract,' said one. 'He had been dead for three days and for three nights, but as soon as they laid the body on the saint's tomb the child arose from death and lived.' He paused for effect, his eating knife poised in the air. 'There were many men who saw it happen and who will swear that it is true. And that is not the only miracle that has been wrought there. The crippled have walked, the blind have been made to see and many who were sick have been restored to health by the love of the martyr.' The friar transferred his knife to his other hand to make the sign of the cross.

'And have you seen any of these things for yourself?' asked Eble.

'Not with my own eyes,' admitted the friar, 'but I have been told these things by people who have themselves witnessed the miracles. And the reports are so numerous that I have no reason to doubt their veracity.' He speared a piece of fish with his knife and looked affronted that his word should be doubted. Eble frowned. He had thought that the problem of Thomas of Lancaster had been resolved by his execution. He had not expected this.

'Saint Thomas was much wronged in life,' said the second friar. 'Take his wife as an example.' He glared in Eble's direction, leaving him in no doubt that he had heard other rumours as well. 'Adultery is a grave sin and yet the saint did not divorce his sinful wife but sought only forgiveness and reconciliation.'

'Oh give me strength!' burst out Eble. 'The man sought no reconciliation, except with his wife's estates. Of course he did not divorce her and risk losing his control over so much money, especially when he had already spent every last silver penny that he owned and was in great debt!'

Eble slammed down his half empty cup and the wine spilled from it like a tide. He stood up and forced himself to walk out of the hall rather than applying his palms to the sides of the two tonsured heads and banging them satisfyingly together. He had no wish to hear any more talk about Alicia. These friars, who claimed to be about God's work, revelled in every sordid story that they heard on their journeys and repeated it more willingly than the gossiping wives on a market day.

He walked without a clear purpose and found himself in the stables where, looking for some task, he picked up a bridle and a cloth and began to scrub. As he worked and his temper subsided he began to think about what the friars had said. The sanctifying of Thomas of Lancaster could only make Alicia's situation worse. Although he did not believe most of what the friars had said, he knew that there would be those who would blame Alicia and who would delight in seeing her brought low — and not least amongst those would be Hugh le Despenser whose ambition was becoming legendary.

As Eble rubbed at the leather, he could not erase from his mind's eye the look on Alicia's face when he had left her. Although he did not regret helping his nephews, he was sorry that she had found it so difficult to understand his dilemma. He had persuaded himself that he was acting honourably by leaving her in the care of John de Warenne, but he was now forced to admit to himself that she was not John's responsibility, but his. He had persuaded her to leave her husband, to leave her manor at Canford and to go with him to Castle Reigate. He had told her that he loved her, and then he had left her. Then he had left again when he knew that she was being brought to York. He looked up as he heard Roger come into the stable.

'Have they gone?' he asked.

'Yes,' said Roger. 'They declined my offer of a bed for the night and have left with a pack filled with food and a purse filled with a donation.'

'May heaven grant them their just reward,' said Eble looking out of the open doorway towards the black tipped mountains, where the Welsh and the wolves ran wild. 'I do not suppose for a moment that it was chance that brought their preaching to our table.'

Roger joined Eble on one of the upturned half barrels that served for seats. 'It seems that the opposition to the king is not entirely finished,' he said.

'It is not so much opposition to the king as opposition to his favourite,' remarked Eble. 'And if only half of what they say about that man is true it will take more than a saint to redeem him.'

'I will not argue about the wickedness of Hugh le Despenser,' agreed Roger. 'It is what prevents me from making my peace with the king.'

'But make peace you must,' warned Eble, 'if you are to hold onto your lordship here. I have no wish to lose another nephew to the axe.'

'But to make peace with the king is the same as making a pact with Despenser,' argued Roger.

'For now perhaps,' said Eble. 'But I have seen the king's favourites come and I have seen them go. None have lasted and there is no reason that Despenser should be any different. Make peace with the king and John de Warenne will help us to hold our lands.'

'Then you do not think there will be another rebellion?'

'We cannot be led by a dead man,' said Eble as he gave the bit a final polish and stood to hang the bridle on its peg. 'And all those, like Roger Mortimer, who might have led another rebellion are either imprisoned or dead. I do not say that there will not be another uprising against the king — but it will not come just yet. And meanwhile we must do what is necessary to protect ourselves.' He looked at his young nephew. 'Do you feel confident enough to hold this castle without my help?' he asked.

'I do not see why not. Are you thinking of leaving?'

'The Earl of Surrey will not grant me indefinite leave,' said Eble, 'and I think it is time that I returned to his service.'

★   ★   ★

'Do you know the penalty that faces a woman who causes the death of her husband?' demanded Despenser as I sat on my hands on the bench at the side of the hall and shook my head mutely as he asked me once again to sign away everything that I owned. 'Death by burning!'

It was high summer. The air was humid and hot and when I closed my eyes I saw flames being kindled around my bound and bare feet and imagined the stench of my own flesh as the blood that poured from my skin was not enough to quench the flames.

'Alicia,' pleaded John de Warenne, 'just sign the document. The king has been more than generous in the manors he has agreed to grant back to you for your lifetime. Put your name to the document and you can leave tomorrow for one of the manors in Lincolnshire. I will even arrange an escort to take you there safely. Surely that is better than being kept here for month after month?'

'Those lands are mine!' I protested, although I knew that my pleading was falling on deaf ears. 'They have belonged to my family for generations. I don't see why they should be taken from me when I have done nothing wrong!'

'You are a stubborn woman!' complained Despenser. He turned to John. 'Perhaps a night in the dungeon will encourage some co-operation,' he suggested.

'My father was the Earl of Lincoln. My mother was the Countess of Salisbury. Why am I to have those titles taken from me?' I asked. I forced the back of my hand to my mouth and bit at my knuckles to prevent my tears. There was no justice in the way this man was treating me. I had done nothing wrong and was being punished for the sins of a husband I had hated. 'I want to see the king!' I said again, although not once had I been allowed even a glimpse of Edward.

'The king is not here. He has gone on a pilgrimage of thanksgiving. The king has been generous in allowing you these lands for your lifetime!' said Despenser as he prodded the document that was becoming grubby with his fingering of it. 'If it had been up to me I would have seen you sent to a convent!'

'And do you think that would be preferable to the fire!' I demanded, looking up at him. It gave me some pleasure to defy him. He had thought that I would sign away everything I had weeks ago and in the beginning, when I had been filled with despair I almost had. But as the days and the weeks passed I continued to refuse.

'Alicia,' said John de Warenne. 'This cannot go on indefinitely. If you do not sign the king will run out of patience and I will no longer be able to protect you. There are other demands on my time; other places where I should be. You have been given generous lands for your lifetime and you will be allowed to either marry at your pleasure or to not marry at all. Think carefully,' he advised. 'It is only land.'

Only land. As if land was of no consequence to a woman. As if a small house in which to live with a dairy and a pen for some geese and a cow or two to give good cream would be enough to compensate me. That and the freedom to marry — or the even greater freedom not to marry, but to live a quiet and lonely life as a widow with only the occasional visitor at my table to break the monotony until I died alone and unloved and forgotten.

'At least allow me to grant Swaveton to the abbey at Barlings so that a mass may be said for my soul,' I asked as the thought of my own mortality overwhelmed me and I could prevent the tears no longer.

'That's more like it,' remarked Despenser as he saw me break for the first time. 'Now we are getting somewhere.'

'Have some compassion,' John told him. He tried to take my hand to offer some comfort but I pulled it away from him. There was only one man who could have offered comfort, but he had left me. He had left me to fight for the lands that belonged to his family and when he went I had not understood. But I understood now. Now I knew how much it hurt to lose everything that parents and ancestors had worked so hard to win and keep.

'She fears for her life,' remarked Despenser as he sat on the edge of the trestle and watched me like a hawk watches a lamb. I wanted to shout that I did not fear him, that all his threats were nothing to me, but I choked on my tears and I was so tired and I knew that it was hopeless. I could not win. There was nothing I could do to keep those lands. I could not beg a horse and don armour and ride into battle against the king and this man. All I had were my words and my will, but I had used all the words that I knew and as I wept I acknowledged that Despenser was right. He had broken my will. He had won.

'Do you have to look so damned pleased?' John asked him. 'At least let her grant Swaveton to the abbey.'

'Agreed,' said Despenser after a moment. He snapped his fingers at a servant. 'Bring the lady's clerk and have him draw up the document. She may sign them both. And if she will sign neither,' he said, 'then she is going to be here for a very long time.'

'Alicia,' said John. 'Alicia, you must sign these documents. I know it seems hard, but I will plead your case with the king and in a while, if you prove yourself loyal, he may soften towards you and return some of them. But he has to show his power. He has to show that Thomas of Lancaster is dead and gone and that he has everything that once was his.'

I shook my head and wiped my face on the hem of my gown. 'Once he has my signature he has no need to keep me alive,' I said. 'How can I believe that I will ever be allowed to leave here?'

John sat down beside me and put an arm around my shoulders. 'Alicia,' he said, 'sign the documents and you can leave with me tomorrow. I am going to Conisbrough and from there I will send you on to Swaveton with an escort.'

'And what then?' I asked.

'I will ensure that arrangements are made to protect you. No one will harm you,' he promised. 'You will be safe.'

'Was Maud de Nerford safe when you left her in her manor house?' I asked. I wiped the last of my tears on the heel of my hand and looked at him. 'You cannot guarantee my safety,' I told him. 'I know that you will try — and I am grateful for what you have done for me. But my fate was written on the day that my father arranged for me to marry Thomas. The wheel has turned at the whim of Fortune and now I am cast down and there is nothing that can be done to raise me up again. When I grant Swaveton to Barlings Abbey I will ask that they bury my body there. It is over now,' I told him.

'Alicia, you must not say such things.' He reached for my hand and I allowed him to hold it. It was warm and strong but it was not Eble's hand.

'Tell Eble that I am sorry,' I said. 'Tell him — tell him that I love him.' I sobbed again. 'And tell him that I understand now how important family lands are, and that I am pleased that his family still has Knockin Castle.'

'Alicia! Stop this, please,' begged John. 'It is not as bad as you think.'

'It is,' I said, taking back my hand and standing up as the clerk came in with his papers and ink. 'I will sign these documents and then I will make my confession, and Hugh le Despenser may do with me as he chooses.'

My hand trembled as I dipped the quill into the ink and wiped it. For a moment my hand hesitated and then I signed my name, the nib scratching at the surface of the parchment as I wrote. Hugh le Despenser moved the document aside and laid a second on the trestle. The sum of twenty thousand pounds in fine to the king for the grant for life of . . . I knew it off by heart, the short list of manors in Lincolnshire that were to be mine, though for how long I was unsure. But at least the monks at Barlings would be paid to pray for my soul, and the souls of my parents and of Edmund, drowned in a well at Denbigh, and John, fallen from a turret at Pontefract. Denbigh, my place of birth, would become the property of the man whose sleeve touched mine as he waited. I could hear his breath. I could smell his scent. In a moment he would point again at the place on the parchment and command me to sign it. I did not give him the satisfaction, but dipped the quill once more and signed my name — Alicia de Lacy — the sometime countess of Lancaster, Lincoln and Salisbury.

'Well that wasn't too hard after all? Was it?' said Despenser after he had witnessed the signature and the seals were pressed into the softened wax. He beckoned to a servant to come forward with wine. He held out a cup to me himself. 'I trust you will not throw it in my face,' he challenged.

'I would not waste such good wine on you,' I replied after I had taken it and sipped its contents. 'You are not worth it.'

It was only a small victory and he laughed as if he did not care, but he did not have me taken back to my chamber straight away.

'I have made arrangements with the sheriff of Lincolnshire to watch carefully over your welfare,' he told me. 'You need not fear another abduction.'

So I was still to be a prisoner, I thought. He would set men to watch me to make sure that no rebels or Contrariants gathered at my door.

'Your concern is touching,' I replied.

He went to the trestle and returned with another parchment which he held out to me.

'What is this? My death warrant?'

'It is permission to marry again, to whomever you choose,' he said. 'Although I doubt that there will be many suitors who will seek you out. A woman with little property and well past child-bearing years does not have the advantages that were yours when your father arranged your marriage to Thomas of Lancaster.'

The words stung more than if he had slapped me and I raised a hand to my cheek, almost expecting to feel the heat of the blow. But what hurt most was the truth of what he said. Who would want me now? I had nothing to offer.

When Eble le Strange had fallen in love with me I had been the high born lady on the white horse and he had been the lowly squire.

His love had been a courtly ritual and even though, for a while, we had made it real it was an ethereal thing; like the sound of his singing it had vibrated in the air between us then faded without a trace. What use was that love to him now? He had need of a young bride who could bring him land. He had need of a girl who was young and fertile enough to provide him with heirs. I stared into the wine in my cup and saw a dim reflection of the face of a woman who was growing old, a woman who was barren, a woman who had nothing to offer.

'The Earl of Surrey has said that he will see you safely to Lincolnshire,' said Despenser. 'Perhaps you had better make arrangements for your belongings to be packed. He does not want to delay.'

26

Despite what Eble had told Roger, it was not rejoining the service of the Earl of Surrey that was his true purpose for leaving Knockin to ride west. Although he was headed for Conisbrough where he hoped to find his friend, or at least news of him, it was Alicia who was on his mind. He could not spend another day of idleness in his nephew's castle wondering how she fared. And even though she might not welcome him, he had determined that he must find her and try to make amends.

He was thankful that the summer days were long and that it was not quite dark when he reached Conisbrough Castle. He left the horse with a groom, who was still chewing at the supper he had been forced to leave, and ran up the steps to the hall.

'Eble!' John got up from his chair on the dais and came forward to hug his friend. 'I am glad to see you safe and well. Set another place,' he instructed a servant despite Eble's protest that he was not worthy to sit at his lord's table. 'I have spoken with the king and convinced him that you were with me at

Boroughbridge,' he reassured him when a platter had been placed in front of him and a cup filled. 'I would have sent word but my mind has been otherwise occupied — besides I had no great need of you and thought it better if you remained with your nephew a while.' John paused. 'Is he well?'

'He is not involved in the planning of another uprising if that is what concerns you,' said Eble, tearing at the bread. 'Roger will swear his loyalty to the king, for now at least. What do you make of Lancaster becoming a saint?' he asked. 'I could barely fight my way through the crowds around Pontefract.'

'I know. I saw the same frenzy,' said John, scratching his ear. 'Despenser is determined to quell it, but I'm not sure how easy it will be.'

'And Alicia,' said Eble. 'What does she say about it?' He met John's eye as his friend hesitated. 'She is safe, isn't she?' he asked as a panic rose to fill his throat.

'Yes.' John put a hand on his arm. 'Yes, she is safe.' He paused and Eble stopped eating and stared at his anxious face. 'She has lost everything,' he told him. 'Pontefract, Lincoln, Bolingbroke, Denbigh. The king — or more correctly Hugh le Despenser — has forced her to hand over all her lands, including those she held by right of her mother. She has been allowed Swaveton, and a few other manors in Lincolnshire for her lifetime, but that is all.'

'Where is she?' asked Eble, his food forgotten.

'She has gone to Swaveton. I sent her with an escort and they returned to say that she was safe and everything was well. But, Despenser suspects that there are those amongst the marcher lords who would use her as a rallying point for a new rebellion and he has instructed the sheriff to keep a close watch and not allow her to move too far from her home. You must be careful,' said John. 'If you are planning to go to her then ride under my colours. I doubt the sheriff of Lincoln will know your face and he will not suspect if I send someone to check on her welfare.'

'What manner of welcome do you think I will receive?' asked Eble.

'I do not know,' said John. 'She has been through a difficult time and will need some gentle handling.'

'So she still hates me,' said Eble.

'No, she does not hate you. But there are things which need to be said, cracks that must be mended that can be only be repaired by you and her alone.'

'I have not been the hero that she believed me to be,' replied Eble. 'I think that I am better at writing the stories and singing the songs than I am at performing the deeds.'

'We can none of us live up to the example of those heroes,' said John. 'We are all flawed. Though there is some good come out of this,' he added. 'Alicia has been granted the freedom to marry again at her own will. Despenser is convinced that there is not a man on earth who would take on the penniless widow of a traitor — but then he never did believe that a man should act except for his own advancement.'

★ ★ ★

The church at Swaveton was silent, yet it was the silence that reassured me. I had been brought here by my mother when I was a child, still safe within the circle of my parents' love, to visit the burial place of my ancestor Nicola de la Hay. As my mother had prayed before a candle on the altar my attention had strayed to the paintings on the walls and there was one that intrigued me. Now, after saying my own prayers and lighting candles for the souls of the dead, I walked across the quiet space to look at it once more. It was a picture of a huge wheel, and at its centre was the crowned figure of the Lady of Fortune with her arms outstretched along the spokes to turn it around and around. At the top of the wheel was a king, crowned and dressed in vermillion, but as the wheel was turned by the hand of fortune he fell and lost his crown and was brought to nothing.

There were times when it had been whispered that Thomas of Lancaster might become king of England and I his queen, but fortune had turned her wheel and we had fallen — he to his grave and I to impoverishment.

I heard the latch of the outer door being lifted and I turned, expecting to see the priest. But the figure who was closing the heavy door behind him was dressed in the livery of the Earl of Surrey. He began to walk towards me and there was a familiarity in the way he moved and as a beam of sunlight from a narrow window illuminated him I recognised Eble le Strange. For a moment I did not move, wondering if he were some apparition come to haunt me. He paused when he saw me and we stood and stared at one another. He had one hand inside his cloak and my heart began to thump as I feared that he was hurt.

'Eble?' I said. I went to him and touched him, to reassure myself that he was real. A pitiful sound echoed around the church and I stared at his face, afraid that even the lightest touch of my fingers had caused him such pain. But when he moved his cloak aside I saw a tiny kitten cradled in his arm. He held it out towards me and I took it between my hands as its claws scrabbled in the air seeking for security. I sat down on the bench against the wall and put the tiny creature on my lap and stroked its head. It was black except for a triangular patch of white beneath its chin and when it looked up its green eyes locked onto mine and studied me with interest.

'I know it is not a replacement,' he said. 'But I thought that you would like it anyway.'

'Thank you,' I said, looking up at him. 'I did not think that you would come.'

'Alicia . . . ' he began.

'No,' I said. 'There is no need for you to explain. So much has changed.' I glanced up at the painting on the wall. 'They say that you do not know the value of something until you lose it,' I said. 'I think that I did not understand the importance of family lands until mine were taken from me. I understand now why you had to go to Knockin.'

'My decision came at a price,' he said as he watched me fondle the cat.

'I am sorry about your nephew.'

'There was a higher price than that. I made you hate me.'

'I never hated you Eble,' I told him. 'I was angry and disappointed. But now I know that

I expected too much from you. I asked more than you were able to give. I wanted you to be a hero, like Guarin de Metz, and I forgot that what my nurse once told me is true — that those stories are not about real life.'

'I have failed to be the gallant knight who should have ridden to your rescue,' said Eble. 'I was persuaded by John de Warenne to return to the marches and I regret it. I should have stayed in York and tried to help you.'

'And risked losing your head along with your nephew? I do not blame you, Eble,' I said.

'I thought that you would. I thought that you would still be angry. That is why I came with the gift of a kitten. I thought you would not strike a man with a cat in his hands.' He looked rueful but I caught the beginning of a smile.

'I have nothing to offer you in return,' I told him. 'I am no longer the great lady to be loved and admired from afar.'

'Alicia,' he said. I raised my eyes and met his blue gaze. His fair hair was as unruly as ever and I felt the familiar jolt in my stomach that came whenever I looked at him. 'Do you remember the story of the Lady Mellette?' he asked.

'Yes, of course I do.'

'And what did Lady Mellette say when her

uncle asked if there was no knight in Christendom that she would take as her lord?'

'I do not recall.'

'Yes you do, Alicia. She said that of riches she made no account.'

'For truly can I say that he is rich who has that which his heart desires,' I replied.

Eble pointed to the wheel of fortune on the wall. 'Do not only look at those who are cast down,' he said. 'See how those who have begun in a lowly state may rise on the wheel. The putting down of this rebellion is not the end, Alicia. There are too many people who are angry with the king and with his favourites and with the way you, and others, have been treated. The wheel in this picture appears to stand still, but fate only pauses. Things will change. Others will be brought low and those who have had only lowly beginnings may ascend.'

Then he knelt down in front of me and took the hand that was stroking the kitten. He held it firmly for a moment then raised it to his lips. They were soft as they brushed my skin.

'I know that for the present I am only a lowly squire, but, Alicia de Lacy, will you do me the honour of becoming my wife?' he asked.

'Yes,' I said. 'Yes, I will be your wife.' I put the kitten down on the bench. It complained with a loud meow, but I was already in Eble's arms and my face was pressed against his chest and I was safe. And I no longer envied the Lady Mellette. She had Guarin de Metz, but I had Eble and I did not want any other man.

We do hope that you have enjoyed reading
this large print book.

Did you know that all of our titles
are available for purchase?

We publish a wide range of high quality
large print books including:
Romances, Mysteries, Classics
General Fiction
Non Fiction and Westerns

Special interest titles available in
large print are:
The Little Oxford Dictionary
Music Book
Song Book
Hymn Book
Service Book

Also available from us courtesy of
Oxford University Press:
Young Readers' Dictionary
(large print edition)
Young Readers' Thesaurus
(large print edition)

For further information or a free
brochure, please contact us at:
Ulverscroft Large Print Books Ltd.,
The Green, Bradgate Road, Anstey,
Leicester, LE7 7FU, England.
Tel: (00 44) **0116 236 4325**
Fax: (00 44) **0116 234 0205**

Other titles published by Ulverscroft:

AN HONOURABLE ESTATE

Elizabeth Ashworth

England, 1315; Famine and unrest are spreading across the country, and when Sir William Bradshaigh joins Adam Banastre's rebellion against their overlord, the Earl of Lancaster, things do not go to plan. Sir William is lucky to escape with his life after a battle at Preston and, as a wanted man, he has no choice but to become an outlaw. Meanwhile, the lands at Haigh are forfeit to the king, who gives them to Sir Peter Lymesey for a year and a day . . . while Lady Mabel Bradshaigh must make a hard choice if she is to protect her children and herself.